The Sailor's Disquiet

The Sailor's Disquiet

A Novel by Michael Delisle

Translated by Gail Scott

THE MERCURY PRESS

The publisher gratefully acknowledges the financial assistance of the Canada Council for the Arts and the Ontario Arts Council. The publisher further acknowledges the financial support of the Government of Canada through the Department of Canadian Heritage's Book Publishing Industry Development Program (BPIDP) for our publishing activities.

A NOTE ON THE TEXT
Asterisks indicate text that was in English in the original.

Edited by Beverley Daurio
Cover design by Gordon Robertson
Composition and page design by TASK
Printed and bound in Canada
Printed on acid-free paper

1 2 3 4 5 04 03 02 01 00

Canadian Cataloguing in Publication Data
is available for this title.

The Mercury Press
www.themercurypress.com

For J.-F. B.

Table of Contents

Bad Boy

Strictly speaking, the only splotch on my record is Jean-François Vézina-Côté, fourteen years old. I blew off his head. His red head flew up into the sky and landed in a huge blue pine in his parents' front yard. As for fat Asselin, he got away with eight months in a cast, burns and tubes. He's solid, fat Asselin. Obviously, I'm not counting the lawyer on rue Grant; he was already dead in his chair when I fired. And Roch Manseau, who knows if it was my crack with the hammer that did it? I was the eleventh to have a go. When it got to be my turn and I walked up to him, his jaw hung like loose skin under the chin, and his shirt was covered with bits of teeth; for sure, almost, he was dead when I bashed him. Strictly speaking, in the whole picture Jean-François Vézina-Côté is the only little blot. Nothing else comes to mind. But it is always difficult to plumb the depths of a man's memory. Sister Russell says none of us have any idea how great is the mercy of the Lord.

When I climbed up the stairs to Sister's place, I was a cracked shell of a man, my guts had all leaked out. I was covered with sores. And I was wandering aimlessly down the street, being jostled about by the crowd, when in the hubbub, I heard singing. It came from a half-open window above. I heard Sister's voice both as part of the chorus and rising over the chorus. I dragged myself up the steps, one by one, one hand on my knee, the other hand pulling the railing towards me as if it were ship's rigging, yes, heaving myself up toward the psalms coming from the Mission on the second floor. I breathed heavily with every step. And I knew I was old. Finished. An old geezer, his veins clogged with fat. I was turning into the very thing I had always detested. The monster I had spent my life eradicating by blows of the hammer, in the back of my head, or sticks of dynamite in that blimp of an Asselin's car on rue Radisson, a certain May morning. And up the stairs, there, people were singing, I remember as if it were now, nothing is like the first time, they were singing *No Other Help I Know.** They were really outdoing themselves with the chorus *And I say, father, I call you my father,** all the sorrow leaching out of their throats with I call you my father. The magic of those people on the second floor, that magic worked, it released me like getting drunk does. I was covered with red blotches that itched in the encrusted folds of my body. And I struggled up the stairs, wheezing away, one hand glued to the railing, the other pushing down on my knee to get to the landing. I was old and fat, and needed to be alone.

It was on boulevard Saint-Laurent, near Chinatown, where anyone can see, just by looking at the people, that the river is nearby. As I walked, that evening, my nostrils breathed in the ferrous odour of the sea where cargo ships have dipped; just as I was about to climb the steps that led me to Sister Russell's Mission, I got a whiff of air that smelled of paint-pocked metal. And as I hoisted my way up with my heavy body, I exhaled the memories of a kid tossed about by the green waves of the Atlantic.

Sister Russell looked me right in the eye and said: "We were waiting for you."* A man unfolded a chair. Everything that Sister Russell said was aimed at me. You could tell. She spoke of "the cruel truth."* She mentioned the prodigal son and said he was the favourite. His parents, through loving him no matter what he did, became good people. He was, in a way, the chosen one, the one who compelled those around him to commit acts of faith.

Before the end of the sermon, I surprised myself by joining in with the others, punctuating Sister's fine words with hallelujahs. It was spontaneous, spontaneous as a heartbeat, a heart that would, from now on, beat at its own rhythm. Yes, I wasn't the same man any more. The sailor was dead. And with him, the henchman. And with the henchman, the son.

I had heaved my way up to the top and my head was turning. As if I were drowning, I sank into my new life with my blissful smile, my unshaven face, my sticky wounds, the same clothes I'd been wearing for a week, some small change, and, in my shirt pocket next to my heart, safe in its plastic case, a photo from the *Journal de Montréal* of the happy face of Jean-François Vézina-Côté.

I didn't have to do a thing. Nothing. I bathed in the radiance of Sister Russell; the rest took care of itself.

Sister's Mission is on boulevard Saint-Laurent because, as she puts it, that's where the action is. People need her here. Wednesdays, Fridays, and Sundays, she welcomes them, switching from French to English as the mood takes her; she welcomes prostitutes, drug addicts, alcoholics, crooks, homeless teenagers, busybodies, refugees from winter warming up by the stove, and even, it has been known to happen, Catholic priests, who come to hear her.

Her daughters sit ready at the piano and accordion for the songs and psalms. After reading a passage from the Bible, Sister steps up on the platform and starts preaching under a bare bulb. A sharp word. Then another. A brisk sentence, right to the point. Slowly warming up until fundamental truths roll off her tongue like words of fire, like she's in a trance. By the end, her whole body moves in time to the Good Lord's Word. She always wears the same grey skirt, the same brown jacket, regular shoes. It's from her thin hands, her wrinkled face and her grey bun that all the glory radiates. When she's finished, she sits down, blows into her fingers to warm them up, and crosses her ankles.

Then the born-agains bear witness. A former prostitute tells how she went wrong. From the age of five her uncle and father used her to do bad things and paid her to keep her mouth shut. Later, Jesus saved her from vice and hard drugs. Every day, she forgives those who have condemned her, and swears she loves and honours her parents, even if they have disowned her since she chose the right path. She weeps with joy. When she says "the right path" the words flow through us. Hallelujahs rise in unison, spontaneous, all of us swept away on the swell. Then an old crook gets up, lists his heists, and says he will never do it again because the blood of Jesus has washed him clean. It ends with prayers and songs. We fold up the chairs. Wednesdays, the Petersons bring in coffee and cookies.

I have been counted among the faithful, a regular at Sister Russell's meetings for five years now. I haven't missed a single evening. Once a month I volunteer for addressing flyers. On holidays I hand out tracts. After supper, I distribute Bibles in the port. Five years have gone by since I climbed up her stairs and sometimes it still feels like two days. My sores have practically disappeared on my back and legs and I take the Mission steps without flinching. Healed by my redheaded angel, miraculously cured by my cherub with wings of fire.

My room is only a minute from the Mission. I share a kitchen with young Legault. I earn an honest wage, in a tannery, and every day I pray for my boss who can't get through a sentence without taking the Lord's name in vain. Meeting evenings, I get there early to unfold the chairs, and I stay after to put things away.

When I'm not working I read the Bible in my room, hand out flyers and meeting invitations in the street, and when I hear a Soviet ship has docked, I sneak into the port with Bibles in Russian for sailors who want them. No one knows how Communists are dying for the Word of the Lord. Legault holds the box, and I hand out the Holy Book. There's always time to give out a few before getting chased away by the crew master.

Once Legault and I went right up on board with our box. The crew master, a six-foot guy built like a refrigerator, with their typical straw-coloured hair, pounced on me, cursing in his native language. I gave a quick rundown of our basic beliefs, but he didn't understand a word. Filled with the power of the Lord, I, only five feet, four inches tall, took the big guy in my arms and opened my heart: my love gushed out, right through the head of Jean François Vézina-Côté in my pocket, and flowed into the giant's stomach. A miracle, bestowed by my redheaded angel. The crew seemed worried. I have no idea how we looked, me with my head nestled against his heart, and he, arms wide open, stunned. By the grace of Jean-François Vézina-Côté, Babel fell, and, that evening, about ten Russians trooped into the Mission, led by my big blond guy. Honestly, I believe they didn't understand a word, but they sat politely until the very end. Sister inspired them, one way or the other. For sure.

Tonight, for the first time since I clambered up the Mission steps five years ago, Sister Russell feels I am ready, and has invited me to testify at the meeting. I haven't up until now, and no one has forced me. Now the chairs have been unfolded, people are coming through the door, and I am nervous. My hands are sweating and my stomach's churning. I keep going to the men's room, for nothing. My psoriasis itches along my back and inside my thighs. The skin cracks like an ice floe in spring. It's the first my old abrasions have surfaced so virulently.

I, Richard Daudelin, am to testify. To look "the cruel truth"* in the face, as Sister Russell puts it. There are things I've never told anyone, not even Legault in our confidence-exchanging marathons. Some things are hard to remember. Pieces that have fallen out of a picture and landed kersplat on an empty table. A jumble of bits and pieces. A little crab. A stone whitened to chalk in the sun. A light bulb that a cop has placed in my hand. As soon as I close my eyes to think about it, the effort to remember disolves in a beatudinous white light: as if I were praying: I plunge into a sea void of images, and I resurface from this state at peace, washed clean of my wants. And I forget what I was looking for.

Sister Russell stands up on the platform, and her girls strike a chord. That means it's starting.

I am nervous. I don't sing along. I scrape my thumbnail against my worn-down teeth, same as when I was eight, standing in line for the confessional with the other guys at boarding school, nervous, trying to come up with some sins. Rude to my father... Dirty words.... Nasty thought... Quarrels... The end of Roch Manseau. Was that in '57? Roch Manseau, there's a story to show from what depths I've risen.

I was twenty, maybe, and I was already Robillard's right-hand man. Roch Manseau had been playing both sides of the fence for a dog's age and we caught him at it. The hold-up at Belmont Park with the cops waiting, that was him. The still in Farnham, wrecked by the Mounties, him again. He needed to be taught a lesson. Robillard came up with the hammer deal. Roch Manseau was tied to a chair in his garage, and outside Robillard waited with a gang he'd rounded up for the job. It was he, Robillard, who struck the first blow, landing it neatly on the lower forehead where the eyebrows met. He wanted "the rat to cry tears of blood," as he put it later, after several topped-up glasses of rye that still couldn't make him forget how mad he was. He came out of the garage and handed the tool to Birdy Perron who went in and took his turn. Perron, like everyone who went after, took care to close the door behind him. He raised the hammer and came down as hard as he could on the stool's jaw. When he came out of the garage he handed the hammer to the next in line, Léo Lussier. Leo hated him and let him know it. Then Royal Poliquin: kind of holding back. Then Joe Mancini: a strongarm, but almost neutral, just doing his job. And Gerry Frigon and Marc Lussier. Jean-Guy Legris. Bonneau Lapointe. Dan Rhéaume. Frank Rizzo. The guys went at it like they meant it, or in solidarity. Robillard only gave one instruction: aim for the head, don't "water it down." The head. Nothing but the head. From the garage, always the same dull thud of steel hitting bone. Up until the sixth or seventh guy, Roch Manseau screamed, cried, spit out his teeth. Everyone took his turn, from the meanest to the greenest.

We drew lots and fate decided I was eleventh. When someone put the tool in my hand, the handle was hot and damp and curly hair was stuck to the claw. I walked over to Manseau; he stank of blood, rancid oil, and piss. His head was a mess. His scalp was broken right open in places, pushed back in little pleats, so you could see cracked skull. I closed my eyes and hit, hoping not to break through the cranium. The thought of splattering my striped suit jacket made me sick. I felt my way out of the garage, eyes closed not to have to look again.

No one knows which blow actually wiped out Manseau; maybe we're all innocent. Especially Robillard and I, since he was the first and I was last. It's impossible that either of us delivered the fatal one. Everyone went home to his own place after promising to keep his mouth shut. I threw up. Then slept like a log.

But that Aimé Robillard is like the devil himself, as smart as they come. It turns out more than half of the guys involved in the bashing, even including Robillard, were heavily in debt to Manseau, debts now forgotten, you might say. As far as the human element, Robillard stood on principle: it doesn't really hurt when it's a direct blow to the head. The theory gave us something to chaw on.

I was only twenty at the time. More or less. I know that Sister doesn't judge anyone, but I don't think she'd appreciate the Manseau story. It's full of names. That would bother her. Normally you can't use names. You can only speak about yourself, for yourself.

I have to put my finger on what my heart wants to reveal. That's all. That's what I have to do.

There's Mona Novak. She was spared. She's certainly part of my old life. Mona. In spite of the real affection that might have existed between us sometimes, despite the bond between us, despite all the good and bad things you could say about her, she was vulgar. No matter how hard she tried, expensive suits and diction classes, she was cut from the cloth of a five-dollar trick. For sure she's the same as when I last saw her, two years ago, hunkered down in her one-room apartment, wearing bedroom slippers, bald, depressed.

Mona, only the ruby flames of my angel can save you.

Legault says I have the habit of putting my hand on my breast, like a communicant promising to be good. That makes me smile. I don't say anything when he teases me. I just smile. It's true that I often put my hand on my heart. There, in my shirt pocket, nests the photo of Jean-François Vézina-Côté. I close my eyes and say thanks to him. For his guidance. For his providence. For his warmth. I could never thank him enough. Your help is immeasurable, my little cherub. Sister wants me to testify? So be it. Jean-François, you who bathe in the radiance of the Good Lord on High, whisper some words in my ear that will move the hearts of my brothers. I open myself to your grace. It is you who will tell the truth, "the cruel truth,"* in my place.

But, my little redheaded angel, my palms are damp. This isn't supposed to happen. My peace of mind is slipping away.

It is leaking out a crack in the chalice. I am lost, I am falling into the abyss. The end of the world is near, I feel as icy as death. I am in danger. Jean-François, you have to stay with me like a warm breath on the back of my neck.

The very first thing I did, when I was back in my room, was to shave off my moustache. Sister Russell says when we are saved we feel the need to make a sacrifice to the Lord up above. It's natural. Lots of folks stop smoking, drinking, chasing after women. I've been wearing a moustache for more than twenty-five years; I surrendered my old face to the Lord. As the scissors clipped away under my nose, I was suddenly aware, for the very first time, of the presence of Jean-François Vézina-Côté. I could feel the warmth of my dear angel beating about my shoulders; he was blessing my offering. I smiled at him. My tears flowed down over the baby fresh skin on my upper lip. I wiped my face. I was a new man.

I'd gotten my angel's picture a few days earlier. It was the day after the explosion on rue Radisson, and I bought the *Journal de Montréal* and clipped out the picture of the redheaded boy, a school photo they'd published in an inset on page one. I slipped the photo into a plastic envelope, like the ones they give out at the Credit Union to put your bank-book in. I placed my icon in my shirt pocket and I warmed it with my hand to seal the plastic. My hand guided by a force greater than itself.

I have made his image mine. He is always with me, my glowing scapular. If I forget him in my room and he spends the day cooling off in the pocket of a dirty shirt, the hours at the tannery tick by so slowly, and no one could imagine how deeply I suffer. Jean-François Vézina-Côté, your red mark is upon me, I bear the brand of your grace.

At first, on the advice of Legault, the guy in the next room, I found a job at Runik Novelties, an import warehouse. Packing and unpacking all sorts of goods: water pistols from Japan, Rodin thinkers, hippy incense burners; but before long, I had to take a stand. I quit because they wanted me to deal with the contents of a box stamped CANDLES, sent from Los Angeles: I was supposed to package them into lots of six. The candles I'm referring to had an unnameable shape, and I was starting to get principles. The boss said "the dildoes or the door." Nobody stopped me leaving.

Next, I found a job at Westcott Leather, a dilapidated tannery in the east end. I'm still there, unfortunately for Legault, who puts up unflinchingly with the pestilential stink I bring home every day from work. During the hours spent in that sweatshop, my weight drops and my faith increases in leaps and bounds. The bosses put a shower in the changing room, but it didn't help, the smell sticks to the skin. It never goes away. And as far as the so-called shower is concerned, there was more water coming out of the one they had on the *Victoria Marsh* in '53, which isn't saying much. It's a good thing that round about that time the Czech who manages our building, inspired by my ever provident angel, put a brand new bathtub in our bathroom.

It was at Westcott Leather that Aimé Robillard caught up with me.

I was busy with whatever I was told to do when I got there that morning. For an hour I did the knives, then I went over to soaking and drying. Sometimes, for an extra dollar, I would volunteer to unload a shipment of fresh hides, raw pelts crudely skinned, with chunks of flesh and rancid fat still clinging to the derm. Most of the employees were disgusted by the swollen larvae crawling around in the sticky viscosity. Me, in the midst of the stink, I just thought of Job humiliated on his pile of manure, or better, I smiled at the pure pink aura of my cherub. By virtual raising mind over matter, even my psoriasis was almost gone.

I was scraping a pelt when the foreman led Aimé Robillard to my stall. He was wiping the sweat from his forehead and breathing through his handkerchief. I recognized the navy monogram on a corner of the cloth, and the ostentatiousness saddened me. Aimé's expensive tastes came flooding back, all his pride and pomposity. I removed my glove and shook the hand of my old boss, the guy I called Chief for twenty years. Yes, boss. No, boss. My deference made us both feel good.

Aimé Robillard wanted me to go and work for him again; there was a lot to do in the new business. He had inherited a paint factory. In his language, formerly my own, "inheritance" was a euphemism for extortion. Aimé didn't blame me for wanting to lie low for a couple of years after what happened with fat Asselin and Mona, but, in his opinion, to be perfectly frank, enough was enough. I asked him if he was still operating in defiance of the Lord's will, and he looked at me through crinkled eyes, like he did when sussing out a bluff. He checked to see if it was really me without my moustache. I told him Sister Russell was preaching this evening. I've always got meeting announcements on me so I handed him one. Troubled, maybe he even felt sorry for me, he reached for his wallet, but I immediately averted my eyes. It was clear I wasn't interested. Nor was he interested in my flyer.

The reek of carrion was getting to him: he fled and I heard him vomit as he turned into the corridor. He gagged, almost bellowing, between heaves. It surprised me he wasn't any thinner. Aimé was now an old man. He had to find the path of Jesus. I asked my cherub to grant him grace.

Otherwise, my day passed as usual. There wasn't much work to be had in those days, and I can't count the number of times Jean-François Vézina-Côté helped me hang on, in that suffocating tannery.

Evenings, after my tea and macaroni, I read the Bible in the kitchen, or exchange stories with Legault about what happened handing out tracts, about the mysterious ways of the Lord. I can feel Jean-François Vézina-Côté, my intercessor with the Lord on High for my each and every want, deep in my conscience during these evenings, when Legault and I tell each other everything.

Our rooms are smack up against the Mission. The rent is high, but job or not, I've never missed paying on the first of the month. Once I even found the sixty dollars on an evening of the thirty-first, thanks to the providentiality of my angel. The three twenty-dollar bills I needed were all rolled up at the back of the utensil drawer. Legault said they weren't his. Some former occupant must have left them there. I know there's no such thing as luck. Forty paid my share of the rent and twenty went to aid Sister's good works.

Another example of my angel's magic. (Legault and I are always astounded by the way things turn out.) No sooner had we added up the costs for fixing the place than the building was sold to a taciturn Czech who was a renovation maniac. He almost exaggerates, the way he looks after our comfort. My life is full of stories like that since I opened my heart to the mysterious ways of the Lord on High.

If soap is missing, soap appears. Jean-François Vézina-Côté sees to my every little need, the moment I raise my eyes to heaven.

One night we put up a distant cousin of Sister Russell. A dry little old man from Manitoba. After supper, Legault and I prayed with him. Later, maybe he felt obliged on account of our hospitality, he painted us a little portrait of his cousin's life. With hindsight, maybe he embroidered a bit for our sakes. Legault and I felt kind of uncomfortable. Just the same, we were all ears.

As I thought, Ruth Russell had not been educated in a convent. I was sure she was a woman marked by life's tribulations, which made her salvation all the more valuable in my eyes. After a fairly sordid divorce, she left her daughters with her sister-in-law, Mae, a Pentecostal, pure as the driven snow, and started drinking like you wouldn't believe: "bottomless,"* was how her cousin put it. Then, years of homelessness, sharing park benches with fat squirrels, stooping as low as she could go for a bottle of booze, years on the hoof slowly dissolving her pain in a brown paper bag.

One day in Toronto she went into a Chinese restaurant via the alley door. She'd come to beg for food. The Chinese guy, a curt man who rarely spoke, usually gave her something. While he was scraping some leftover scraps off his cutting board, she made for the Ladies' to wash her hands, and there, in the mirror over the sink, she took a good look at herself. She looked herself straight in the eye, not blinking. She took stock of herself. Then, apparently for no reason, she gave herself a slap. A small tap on the left cheek and something stirred inside her. She did it again, but this time, a slap that smarted. A rude awakening. Ruth Russell was coming back to life. With hard smacks on the mug, she mortified herself. Howling with joy, a joy that was greater than any pain. When Sister says "being born again doesn't hurt, to be born again is an act of grace," that's likely where it comes from. The Chinese cook was shocked by her repentance. He stared at her with his mouth gaping open while she pummelled herself and screamed: "My eyes! My eyes!"* She swore she wouldn't stop until the look in those eyes changed.

That's how Sister's rebirth took place. She woke up and realized she had not been put on this earth for itinerance and the life of a derelict. Nor for a bottle of rye. The Good Lord on High had freed her from the yoke of matrimony so that she might spread His Word. When she stopped staring in her mirror, she was able to see deep into the soul of every face that heaven sent her, as clearly as if they had signs hanging from their chins. One line from Sister Russell and your life could topple. From then on, she knew how to use words to knock you down and raise you up again in the spirit of the Lord.

To symbolize her new life, Sister Russell started preaching in the park where she used to bum around. That's where she realized how good she was on a soapbox, the Lord's power passed through her. The rubbies said she had talent; they praised her for her charisma. But for most of them, it didn't amount to sobering up. "Let's hear it for Ruthie," they hooted, not really listening. She got mad. "Slap yourselves out of it,"* she yelled, and headed for Montréal. She sent for her daughters. The sister-in-law, Mae, said they could come.

The cousin finds Sister Russell's French greatly improved, but, according to him, it's in English that she's the most natural.

These revelations had bothered us. We prayed for Sister Russell. We owed her so much. She is our beacon in the storms of life. Jean-François, his wings folded like hands, prayed with us, his head bowed in the very centre of my being.

I have already thought about making amends with fat Asselin. Sister Russell had spent a month talking about "rendering unto Caesar the things that are Caesar's," and it so happened that the payment of debts was, by a sort of unavoidable coincidence, on the conscience of a good many folks at the Mission. Three years had passed since the explosion of the dynamite that I'd put under the hood of his Cadillac, the shock attenuated by the still-open doors, that's what spared him. Besides, I admit, I'd botched the job.

Just passing by was Jean-François Vézina-Côté, a red-headed boy, my eternal angel, who, as luck would have it, had put down his bicycle to lean his head against the hood of the car in who knows what childish game. They said that the top half of his body was blown to bits and there were no identifiable remains, but the newspapers lie. I know that the head blew off nice and neat, and that it landed miraculously intact in the blue fir.

Fat Asselin, still kicking, spent the winter in intensive care getting reconstructed. I felt I owed him an apology.

I waited for him at the exit of a jewellery wholesaler, and I arranged it so I ran into him on the sidewalk. He was hobbling. Politely, I said, "Monsieur Asselin, I'm the guy. I'm the guy who blew up your car." He pushed me out of his way quite roughly. He hadn't recognized me. Not so much because my moustache was gone, I realize, but because I didn't go about it the right way. He probably took it for a bad joke. Too bad. I did what I could.

My visit to Mona's didn't work out much better. By some coincidence (but, my red angel, does coincidence exist?) her address turned up on Sister Russell's mailing list. I usually volunteered for addressing Sister's flyers. That's how I found out that Mona had returned to live in her old neighbourhood, in a basement apartment in a building on rue Guilford near the Laurier métro station.

From the sidewalk I caught a glimpse of her, blurred, through her screen, with her sky blue bathrobe, slippers and her coffee mug. She was watching TV standing up. She was wearing a beige turban. So it was true about her hair. If she hadn't stayed inside thirty seconds longer to touch up her lips or eyelashes, she'd have been in the car too; she might not have had the same luck as her old Rémi. She was bald from terror. And nerves.

I knocked at her door and the sound of the TV was turned down immediately. She asked who it was. I said, "Mona, it's me," and I could see the Judas hole darken as she approached. I smiled. She started to scream with all her might, with her hoarse voice. In her frenzy, she bumped into furniture, knocking everything over. The neighbour opened his door a crack on the chain, and watched. Mona was screaming so loud. I gave up the idea of seeing her. I was disappointed.

Sister has high expectations and that weighs on me. She already pictures me, standing up at the meeting in front of the centre aisle, unravelling my tale. She'll know if I make it up. Or hold back. I have no trouble talking to Legault. But the idea of bearing witness from the platform under her shrewd eye, that makes me nervous.

The sermon moves right along. Which doesn't help. I grow hot and my skin itches in the middle of the back, where I can't reach to scratch. Oh, little cherub, would that you had fingernails? Would that you had fingernails!

I was seventeen when I boarded the train for Halifax. My father, a big man square as a doorframe, opposed my departure. He said I was gifted and the merchant marine would distract me from what I was meant to do in life. Talent meant at least a lawyer, at worst, a journalist. It almost came to blows. I won. I climbed up on the roof, crossed my arms, and threatened to jump if he kept on harrassing me about continuing studying. Seeing me up there outlined against the sky, he gave in. He knew I meant it: I have a morbid fear of heights.

I accepted his offer to accompany me to the station, and we sat on a wooden bench surrounded by khaki trunks, colourless nuns, and schoolboys in their Sunday best playing tag, neither of us speaking until we heard my train whistle. Maybe there was a word of caution from him, saying for the nth time that all I would learn at sea was how to bob and float, nothing, in short, that might contribute to creating our homeland. Catholic, powerful of mind and body, my father was obsessed with land. Bobbing and floating? I couldn't help smiling at that, coming off my watch in the boiler room. I know my father was a good man. His goodness spread out over everything. A hard man to flee.

On the station platform, before I went aboard, he took me in his arms and, I remember, I looked ridiculous. I was ashamed of my squat body, lost in his ample embrace.

I did some time on a collier, the *Victoria Marsh*, a rusty hulk that turned round and round in the Maritimes. On that job, I kept the furnaces full, shovelled coal, knocked out a rat, anointed the pistons with a greasy mop and learned to bellow, because in the belly of a boat there is no other way to make yourself heard. I took salt pills and picked away at a pile of black boulders beside an inferno that roasted everything that went near it. Listening to the rhythm of the waves dully slapping against the hull, I came to understand that water is an infinite mass. Infinite and evil. It's enough to drive you crazy, the interminable beating and the sharp smell of the air mixed with sweat and coal dust.

Evenings after my shift in the boiler room, I coughed up black stuff and blew black snot out of my nose. My father was a hard man to get away from, but on the *Victoria Marsh*, in the very bottom of the hold, I managed, for a time.

Then, I did night watches on ancient old tubs where it was still the same coal, salty rags and abuse by the second engineer, who clunked me on the back of the head because the boiler thermometer shot up too high.

Then, on my last freighter, the *Ermitage*, I thought I'd reached the promised land: I was a deckhand.

The *Ermitage* was a modern ship which transported construction wood to the Caribbean and returned home loaded with green molasses and a hold infested with scarabs solid as toys. No more soaked rags around the forehead to prevent blistering. No more salt pills to keep me from fainting. No grey seas. I was a deckhand on my way to Cuba and I was on day watch.

The *Ermitage* was supposed to mark the end of my trials, but exactly the opposite took place. The *Ermitage* turned out to be the epitome of my troubles. The day crew had a master by the name of Antonio Hamel.

I was on deck getting a breath of air when he walked up to me with a smile on his face. It was the first day of my new contract and I was in love with life: the sea smelled good, our load of blond lumber oozed its sap, our ship's stern trailed its perfect wake. I took the wind in my face like a figurehead, my hands firmly agrip of the railing. A real man. The spray and the iodine were cleansing my soot-clogged pores. That's when I heard Hamel. He called me by name.

I turned to face him and I didn't like the way he was smiling. He spoke.

Antonio Hamel had known my father when he was young, a fellow union member at *La Presse* newspaper. They were good friends, a bond of mutual respect. The chief electrician, Hamel added in adopting a confidential tone, also had a high opinion of my father, who helped him get a summer job when he was fourteen. It seems that every time the name of the great union militant is mentioned, this chief electrician hastens to praise his generosity.

And I should know that getting hired on the *Ermitage* was not unconnected to the friendship between Hamel and my father. There you have it.

He conjured one memory after another, and with each I grew weaker, as if, with every anecdote, he drew a pint of blood from me. He was inexhaustible. Seeing that I was staring at the sky, he named the different cloud formations, pointing out their resemblances to things as they changed shapes. If I looked down at the sea, he spoke to me about the bottom of the ocean. People had always thought that the ocean floor was as smooth as a dance studio's, but, on the contrary, the Swedes had just proved this wrong. Hamel knew everything. I would have liked to put my hands over my ears. I sat on a winch, arms crossed, and after a bit he went back inside. I remained, hunched over, my face frozen.

We tossed. The sea was unappeasable, never calm, always stirring. Nobody understood perpetual motion, not even the Swedes. The sea foamed on every side like an uncontrollable emotion, and I, hunkered down between wheels, felt as rigid as a schoolboy who has just discovered he's flunking out. No matter what I did, I would never reach the big leagues. No matter what. The sea and its bottomlessness would get the best of me.

From there on in, I was known from the captain to the kitchen boy as the son of my father, and I got what you might call special treatment.

It was on the *Ermitage* that I met Grégoire, a cook who, for the past twenty years, had only slept one hour a night. It is strange to think we never saw each other again after that time in Havana.

My angel, you remind me of things so long past. Where are you taking me? And if you can just calm the sting of my sores as we go, I thank you.

Everything about Grégoire was oversized: his nose, his lips, his eyes, his ears, his hands. Like a study in clay. He walked heavily, with the unruffled stride of a rescue dog. Among the sailors, it was rumoured that he could bend an iron bar with his hands. That made him smile, but he never denied it.

My cherub, why remind me of Grégoire just as I am about to testify?

The truth. This strong man slept next to me. I was

impressed by him from the first night. He wore an undershirt loose enough so I could see perfectly well, on his breast, a heart on a bed of thorns, dripping blood, and I thought to myself: this is a good man. I fell asleep, feeling safe and sound

It wasn't long before being under Grégoire's wing seemed more bearable than Antonio Hamel's patronizing provocations, not to mention the chief electrician's attempts to make me shape up. Grégoire let me be, asked nothing of me, and answered all my questions. At worst, he found that I spoke well and it was my responsibility to make good use of this way I have with words. I tolerated it, hardly ever over-reacted.

The first day, in the streets of Havana, I let him lead me around. The city was as animated as a pagan festival, but I plodded along. Dragged my feet, a little. Worn out from the job, as usual. The public squares and arcades were a festival of colour. Lurking in dark doorways, lost women grinned, lascivious, lips pushed out in the form a heart. They wiggled their hips, staring us right in the eye, or else they grabbed one of their breasts as if offering it to us. A boy half-hidden in the shadows of some columns furtively bared his brown member, murmuring "Cigarros?"

Grégoire told me there were diseases that could blind you. He sounded convincing. It wasn't so long ago, he said, that syphilitic sailors were smothered in their sleep, an act of charity, and thrown overboard. They were registered as lost at sea. Period. His stories frightened me. All the colonial façades looked like brothels.

Around the corner of an alley, a bunch of American revellers came out of an establishment. Their drunkenness was catching and Grégoire mingled with the group. I followed along into an ordinary rum joint where a fan was turning lazily. They were playing a high-spirited scratchy tune of the sort that the Americans ground out ten years back to entertain the soldiers. Grégoire and I drank rum from square glasses held in our fists. Glass after glass, until the rum tasted like water.

Then, nothing.

One thing is certain: the next thing I remember is telling Grégoire I am not going back to the *Ermitage* with him. I will not make the return trip. Cuba was dirt cheap and I could easily see myself hanging around the island for the next twenty years. I'm sure he wasn't too happy. But then...

When memory resists, I don't insist.

My wooden chair squeaks, its screws are loose. I'm afraid it will give way, crash to the floor, interrupt the sermon, and everyone will look around to see where the racket's coming from. Sister is in full flight with a parable. She gestures as she speaks, confidently. But I feel far away. You might say I no longer absorb her words. My palms are wet, my thighs burn.

My turn is coming.

My eyes are red. It's the filings from sharpening the knives at the tannery. They grate on the cornea, and my lids get infected at the drop of a hat. There's no point putting in drops, they only make the iron dust rust. Sometimes, the filings also make my nose bleed when I blow it. The boss says protective masks just cost money for nothing. I don't worry about it. If there were some reason to worry, my cherub is there to warn me, or better, to take me out of harm's way. When I knocked on the tannery boss's door, he was only looking for someone for three months and I'm still there today. That shows how much he appreciates me. As far as money goes, it's minimum wage, and that doesn't look like it's going to change.

At first, the boss swore every second word; now he doesn't as much. I think my example has shown him why taking the Lord's Name in vain doesn't help a thing. When His Name pops out of your mouth, it is preferable to be calling on Him for help.

Wings of beauty, glorious shining love, my thoughts rest on you and I am transported. Then you descend onto me and the lake becomes calm and cool. This I know, my angel, and I declare it: your name, Jean-François Vézina-Côté, is a prayer.

Not counting his long thin legs and his tapered fingers, Aimé Robillard is obese. You can see him coming, his long form, topped by a thatch of silver hair, makes the hard bulge of his belly less noticeable. I checked him out carefully before approaching. He was wearing a short-sleeved white shirt, as usual. His braces, which he likes to stick a thumb behind, gaped, as usual, around his fat breasts. The man who was sucking, as was his habit, the end of a very pricey cigar, still had the air of being totally in control, a man who decided fast and right. I liked his cool ways.

You could smell the pommade he used to paste his silver hair behind his ears, and his neck was bathed in an eau de cologne that smelled strongly of evergreen. His shoes were impeccable: someone bent over and shone them daily. His heavy, sanguine cheeks were shaved by a barber, weighty cheeks that grew longer with their weight when he bent his head to forge a signature or to calculate, long into the night, the columns of debt he owed to a testy loan shark. Aimé's mouth was slack, always agape, and his breathing was wheezy.

Decked out in a shiny suit, he seemed as solid as a hundred-year-old tree. At the slightest pretext, he'd flash a huge wad. We called him "Chief."

I found him relaxing to be with.

Things clicked instantly between us. My slightly out-of-date Latin look, which I had when I returned from Cuba, made him smile. Before I knew it, I was his right-hand man. A nice cozy place to be. In less than a month he was already saying I should come and live with him, his wife Laurette, and his kids. I had my own room, and I had the key.

He had a big modern bungalow, faced with fake stone, alternating with rows of bricks, long and thin as sticks. The garage was double. Behind was the swimming pool, shaped like a giant kidney. The main point of interest in the front yard was a fountain in the middle of a rock garden that went right up to the edges of the corner lot. It looked spectacular; that was the whole idea. The house was set considerably farther back than the neighbouring houses. It looked like the manor of an estate, plunked down between two ordinary front lawns.

The chief wanted something? He only had to ask, and I left his side long enough to give the order. The henchman's job is a breeze. "The fool is the butt of people's jokes," I told myself, "but he lives in the castle."

I didn't get to be his associate without a little rite of initiation. The chief had borrowed a five-figure amount from a lawyer who was demanding payback with exponential interest rates. The chief explained the situation to me, handed me his hardware and the lawyer's address. All I had to do was go there at eleven o'clock in the evening, shoot him down, and return home as if nothing had happened. We'd have breakfast as usual with Laurette and the kids.

I know, red angel, I should have fled on the spot. I was so nervous my stomach ached. I could have taken off, yes, it crossed my mind, but now I was a guy with tailor-made shirts, clean. I liked that. The only other thing I knew how to do was work on ships, you see, and, as far as I could recall, you get dirty on boats.

I sidled up to the study window of the lawyer who lived, that much I remember, on rue Grant in Ville Jacques-Cartier. He was sitting there at the appointed time, just like he was supposed to, bent over his work, under the light of a desk lamp. I was shaking like a leaf. I aimed the chief's gun at the lawyer and pulled the trigger. I raced back home and was sick as a dog. I didn't sleep a wink, played solitaire until dawn. I had finally dropped off when Aimé came into my room; he took his gun, unscrewed the silencer, and fired two shots toward the ceiling. The piece was loaded with blanks. He broke into a booming laugh at my stunned expression. Aimé had taken care of the lawyer himself an hour before I got there.

Two days later, the newspapers ran an article about a

lawyer struck down by a heart attack at his home. An ordinary heart attack. I never knew how Aimé did it. He threw me a look and exploded with laughter at the thought of me knocking off a dead man.

I believe Robillard loved me. With me in his life, his enterprises gradually— how can I put it— had a diminished margin of error. There were more floating card games, more scandal sheets, more loaded municipal elections with a ballot box substitution system Robillard liked to brag he'd figured out by himself. We organized fake lotteries, set up stills, loan sharked. Before turning in for the night— not that I'm nostalgic, but I have good memories of my years with Robillard— we had a kind of sweet-dreams ritual where we sat at the table with a bottle and cigars and hatched the wildest schemes for making a killing, the cutest frauds. There were lotteries where I showed up disguised as a miserable wretch and claimed my winnings, to the touching applause of the suckers who lost. Or we would slouch in our car and watch people arrive at a deserted parking lot for roller-skating lessons that would never take place. We peddled a *Mycology Course* by correspondence to people so impressed by big words that they paid their deposit without knowing what the course was about. We snickered like teenagers as our imagination ran away with itself. Our crazy laughter ricocheted late into the night.

My most frequent job, and I liked it, and it wasn't reprehensible, was the Chinese run. Robillard showed me a way to get over the American border without going through Customs. I could pack up to eight Chinese into my little van like sardines. Each one was allowed to take a bag of clothes, a box, no more. Once I thought it would be fun to take Mona along on the Chinese run, but it made her too nervous. She smoked like a chimney and scratched her hands until they bled. She saw Customs officers behind every tree, in every field, under the snow. Poor Mona!

She and I stuck it out just the same for fifteen years, until she met the fat jeweller.

It was an acquaintance of Robillard stole the sticks of dynamite for me, a very amenable guy. His wife had cheated on him, too, and he knew exactly what I was going through. When it happened to him, he had his wife's legs broken, but that was too paltry for Mona, too much of a drag. I wanted something fast and clean. That guy knew someone who was the security man at a construction site in Boucherville, and he could help himself to whatever he wanted. Ceramic bricks for his bar, windows for the cottage, sticks of dynamite for fishing. It was he who explained how to wire the sticks. I guess I wasn't listening.

When all's said and done, I'm glad Mona didn't go up in bits that morning.

Jean-François Vézina-Côté, my beautiful angel who no longer has to suffer, who never suffered, who stands in witness of what eternal life will be for each of us, I give thanks to you every hour of the day.

Sister is inviting those who wish to testify to come to the front; she looks right into my eyes like on the first day when she said, "We are waiting for you."* My sores are on fire, the pain is radiating into my muscles and bones. It's unbearable.

An effeminate adolescent promptly gets up and stands front and centre. He uses such vague terms to speak of his life that nobody can figure out what sins he is repenting. You have to guess. Then again, you'd have to want to. Furthermore, he doesn't have much to disclose. And I thought I still had some time.

Let's go, my downy angel, Jean-François, my beacon, take my hand, open my heart. Speak through me, reveal everything. "The cruel truth."* I await your words.

My psoriasis has never been worse, not even the day Manseau spit out his teeth, or the day Asselin blew up. I thought this curse was gone forever, that I was over suffering. But it's starting to drive me crazy.

I would cry, but the tears don't come.

I could jump into a frozen lake.

When the young man has finished, a moment passes; then I get up. On the way to the platform, I run a finger over the backs of chairs. Affecting nonchalance. A way of putting off, even for a second, the moment when I stand up there under the bare light bulb.

Everybody's gaze will be fixed on me.

In front of Sister Russell, I pull myself up short. She looks different somehow. Something has changed. Her religious demeanour is the same, with her hands hidden, muff-like, in the arms of her jacket, her head bent... but this woman is not Sister Russell!

In a sudden rush of heat, Jean-François Vézina-Côté reveals the reason for my alarm. He reveals it and I can't believe my eyes. It's Sister Russell's crossed feet. Sister Russell has new shoes! In shiny leather. With little raised heels. Since the first day I met her, five years ago, Sister Russell has always worn the same grey skirt, the same brown jacket and flat-heeled shoes that she got resoled every fall. Today, Sister Russell has bought herself new shoes. Shoes that glimmer in the light, and, what's more, make her look taller!

I move closer. I see them clearly, and I know only too well what they mean. They twinkle and glimmer under the ceiling lightbulb. For everyone to see. The trap door of my soul falls open and my mettle falls out.

Each of Sister Russell's new shoes have two eyelets trimmed in gold.

Beautiful angel, purity personified, how I wish I'd never seen them.

I stood up there in front of everyone, glued to the spot as the moments ticked by, trying to find my tongue, to come up with something to say. I could hear them breathing in the audience, the floor cracking, people fanning themselves with song sheets. I stared at my feet.

From the corner of my eye I see the golden eyelets on Sister's shoes. I never approved of the showiness of those Hollywood-style evangelists. How can I ever trust Sister again, when she adorns herself in such patent luxury? What a display! These things are a sign, everybody knows it. I'm not making it up.

I hear Sister Russell say, cool and calm, "Perhaps some other time, Richard?"* I go back to my chair. Nobody says a word.

I give her the benefit of the doubt— I stay to fold the chairs. That's when, amid the clatter of putting things away, I hear a voice saying Sister Russell has made cassettes of her sermons. Moreover, it's certain that the Mission is moving to

Longueuil, to a sort of empty manor on boulevard Therrien. Sister will make the announcement at the next meeting.

I know that place: it's a twenty-room mansion.

I return to my room, furious.

I undress as best I can. When my lesions rub against things, they crack and bleed. I thought they were over, those days when I slept in blood-spotted sheets. I'm bleeding again. It's going to be a rough night. Tossing around. The wind blows, whistles, outside the window, and in the street the amber light of the streetlights casts shadows as weird as in a fairy tale about witches. I throw my pillow, I pull at my undershirt. I kick the furniture, which I haven't done in ages!

I can't get into my evening prayer. I can't get hold of myself. With my face in my pillow, I think of Sister Russell. I look into the future and what I see is hideous: Sister Russell reeking of Chanel No. 5, Sister Russell pausing in front of jewellery stores, trying on rings with huge stones, big heavy gold things. What's happened to Sister Russell happens to all the preachers who start out with pure souls. The first year, they burn with the passion of their message, making countless numbers repent. Ten years later, more like eight years on the average, they're "on the road" in a seventy-five-thousand-dollar trailer, wearing, and this is what gives them away, a diamond ring. A big one. That's always the sign. A big diamond ring. Sister Russell has failed to avoid the trap of going commercial. The devil has crept into her heart and she has let him corrupt her. She's starting to take shortcuts, she's getting soft. She closes her eyes to the very things she used to condemn. She's working on her image. She has ambitions. Like Mona. Exactly like Mona Novak! She wants to go out covered in glitter, and conquer the world. That's what she's up to: she wants to be seen!

Okay, let her have it all. Let her make cassettes of her sermons. Let her snazzy life style take over. Let her wallow in chinchilla, if that's what she wants.

I'll never get to sleep in this state. I'm going to Sister Russell's and demand that we talk. I'll let Jean-François speak. "The cruel truth"* will be revealed.

As I put my clothes back on, I examine my sores. In a few hours, my psoriasis has returned in all its glory. Pink patches. Red patches. Mona Novak was a prostitute who got what she deserved, but, I swear, she was the only woman who never turned down her nose at the lesions on my body. She could have become a familiar face on TV, had everything it took, except luck. Still, with the help of a dry martini, there were evenings when she was queen for a moment, and she made the most of it. Mona...

After the blast on rue Radisson— and it's one hundred per cent sure she knew who was behind it, knew I hadn't forgiven her for leaving me for a fence with a charm bracelet, after the explosion she lost her hair and fell into a serious depression. Too bad for Mona, but she really asked for it. All and all, I'm glad she wasn't in fat Asselin's car when it blew up. She was forever primping, you always had to wait for her, that's what saved her. The only person in the vicinity of the bomb was the fat unkillable Rémi Asselin. And my little cherub, with his head lying on the hood, my little cherub, transmuted into light, for the better of all.

I'll speak my piece to Sister about the cassettes, about the new shoes. She'll take it without saying a word. She always does that, crosses her arms and waits until you've unloaded. I'll warn her about the diamond rings before the year is up. I'll mention the expensive trailer. I know she will keep her mouth clamped shut until she puts a stop to our conversation with a dry "So be it!"* Cut and dried, that's her style.

It won't do any good. She doesn't deserve it. I might as well go back to bed.

Tomorrow I'll quit my job, and I'll hit the road in my bunged up old van. I'll move on. Period. Fifty, oh red head of my beautiful angel, is not the age of retirement, especially if, each day, you tread the path of the eternal one.

I'll drive straight across Acadia. They say there are Quakers in the Maritimes who have such a pure way of living, they make all their clothes from scratch. Everything in linen. They live on modest farms with chickens and sheep. They live from the sea as well. As much cod as you want.

Hard and dry is Sister Russell, who has not lived close to the sea.

The time it takes to tell my boss at the tannery and pack a suitcase and I'll be in my van en route to the lower Saint Lawrence.

In Havana, I remember, there's a cemetery where the tombstones are topped with crosses white as chalk in the sun, where a young Cuban woman lay whose tomb is covered, good times and bad, with fresh flowers, offerings and votive trinkets. A bit of folklore that has given me many a nightmare. A tale I have wept over, often got drunk over. So much, in fact, that I finally made up my mind that the woman whose body lay under such a weight of gifts never existed. I erased her, a matter of survival. Jean-François Vézina-Côté, little cherub with the orange halo, how many years went by before the story of this dead woman came back to me?

What do you want to know about her?

A child your age guided me among the tombstones for ten cents, under a burning hot sun. He knew nothing about dates or numbers, but he talked enthusiastically in his broken English, and the more lively he became, the more I sank into my passive state, delighted by his performance. He made me smile. When we came to the tomb covered with flowers, I asked him who was buried there. He whispered: "Santa Maria!" and he crossed himself solemnly, rapidly. Then he began recounting.

A long long time ago a woman died. She was called Mary like the Blessed Virgin. Her heart had stopped during pregnancy, her belly was as huge as that. She was mourned, her coffin was nailed shut and they buried her immediately under the stone marker before the body decomposed in the heat. During the night, Mary appeared in the dreams of several women in the city. She knocked at their doors. She wanted to come in. She held a message folded in her hand. The next day the women revealed their dreams to each other, and the coincidence made the authorities decide to open Maria's tomb. They did it without letting another minute go by.

The miracle they uncovered dismayed them. In her dress, covered with blood and raised up around her waist, the remains of Maria held her baby in her arms, on her breast. Her womb had automatically pushed it out, and the baby, in the terrible darkness, had somehow groped its way to its mother's breast. They closed up the tomb again and said endless masses; to this day they say masses for her. And since this time, women who cannot conceive kneel at the foot of the tomb to pray for fertility. And Maria's baby, like the baby Jesus, answers their prayers.

The little Havana boy was fidgeting, and I smiled, wondering what could possess him to invent such a dark tale. But, I'm telling you, I didn't sleep well after that. The bit of folklore had worked its way into my heart, and, as soon as I was on the verge of sleep, I became that baby, eyelids still glued shut with mucus, turning towards the light to cry out against its violent brightness, to begin to live at last. My eye grew dim trying to see what lay beyond its narrow slot, seeking out a ray of hope, maybe even a path among all those that destiny offered. When I grow up, Mama, I will be a fireman, and you will see me step into the flames as cool as a salamander to save entire families, entire families will be saved by me and I will ask for nothing in return. Then my eye closes again and my cheek seeks the nipple. I am nothing but a twitching mouth with no other desire than to suck. I reach the breast, under the damp cotton, and die at once. I snuggle into the cold flesh, and it's there, lying on her dead body, it's there that things take a turn for the worse. In its wooden box, my baby's soul does not rise up. It clings, is mired, in my mother's putrid flesh. My soul and hers are one. Nauseous, century after century.

Under the ground, under the sky over Havana, a heart beats. The island women feel it, know it and come from everywhere to ask to be blessed with a pregnancy, to give thanks for an easy birth, or simply to worship.

Me, I am an old man in his fifties, cramped, as it were, in my bunk, dreaming like a martyr that I am suffocating. Dreaming my tomb is being visited by women.

I might as well get used to it: I'll never again see Sister Russell again, any more than I'll see Mona Novak. What do I need them for? Ever since his head flew off, I have my angel, Jean-François, all to myself. He flutters in my warm centre and my heart lightens when I think of his orange hair.

I float.

Over Cuba. Over the sea. And suddenly I see the dark where there should be light atop the mast of the *Ermitage*. I see a light bulb. The hand that holds it out like a proffered apple. A bulb in the hand of the striped sleeve of the crew master.

Memory's fog's rising.

On the *Ermitage*'s deck, the crew master, Antonio Hamel, his ribbons flashing, held out a box of bulbs. I am supposed to scale the centre mast to replace the burnt-out lights. Normally, I'd have waited until he turned his back, then delegated the task to the next down from me in rank, or else I'd have asked Grégoire to climb up there for me, he was good at everything, my Grégoire, everything, bar nothing, and he'd have done it, and I'd have gone quietly back to swabbing, but

Hamel, after handing me the fresh box of bulbs, stood there, grinning and waiting for me to scale the very highest mast on ship. The highest one of all.

Hamel had taken it on himself to be in charge of my initiation, and had chosen a day when it was really blowing up for my baptism by cloud, and, I, hamming Mr. Confident in front of the others, put my foot on the first rung of the mast.

And, I tell you, I climbed!

The *Ermitage* was pitching and tossing. Below were blue-green whitecaps as far as the eye could see. The wind was deafening. If I had relaxed my grip even for a second, I'd have blown away like a piece of paper, down into the sea, tossed about on the swell, pulled down into the troughs of the waves.

I'm up there, almost as high as the burnt-out bulb at the tips of my fingers, but my fear of falling makes me gasp for breath, my arms are trembling. Like all sailors, I know neither how to dive nor swim.

The ship is rolling harder. It pitches terrifyingly. Each heave of the hull creates, at its peak, a dizzying curve. The mast vascillates like a pendulum gone wild. I am boiling with anger. Nobody had the right to order me to do this. Nobody!

When I reach out my arm to undo the burnt-out bulb, a sudden jerk sweeps me backwards, and with my arms clinging for dear life to the ladder, I see my feet floating in thin air. I see nothing but the sea, as if looking through a wide angle lens. Nothing but the foamy swell. And the monstrous ocean swamping the *Ermitage*, and men, one by one, being swept off and sinking, exhausted, in the green sea. I hug the mast with all my might. With the strength of ten men. I am paralyzed with fear.

Grégoire had to climb up and peel off my locked arms. I believe he laughed. He was calling, shouting my name right in my ear, but the wind made him seem far away.

On the deck, the sailors were laughing, their hands on their hips. What made these men so sure of themselves?

Later, I remember the nurse handing me a cup of strong coffee, saying I had slept long enough. A long time. They said I was delirious for two days, sedated to the gills. I gripped my hot cup with both hands. The freighter had been in dock already for six hours and they were just finishing the unloading. I could hear the Spanish spoken by the Cuban dockhands.

I went down into Havana, and I walked through the streets, on the heels of Grégoire who wanted a drink, dragging along behind him, a sleep-sodden soul yanked too soon from its torpor. I grumbled; I wanted to sleep more. In a rudimentary bar I consumed enough drink to swear to Grégoire that I would never again step onto the *Ermitage's* deck. The more he protested, the more determined I grew. He gave in. I left him sitting there, disappointed and possibly a little irate.

I let myself go. The sun tanned my skin, faded my psoriasis. I floated around on glasses of rum.

It's back, the terror I felt on top of the mast. Back.

I can't sleep, lying in my bunk, alone like in my youth on the boats. When the mattress used to squeak in the bunk above because a sailor was polishing his rod to help him sleep, I would drift off, giggling to myself. I am an old man now. I've passed the half-century mark and I am alone between the sheets, like in the old days at sea. I will dream that I still know how to raise my fists and fight, I'll get over-energetic and it will ruin my sleep. Tomorrow, I'll get up beat and bloated.

Legault has come in. He pauses outside my door, puts his ear against it to see if I am awake. In a minute he will go off to bed.

The roomer next door is noisy, puttering around, making small repairs. It's the first time I've noticed him moving around in there. The noise blends with the hum of the traffic below. The melody of motors. People laughing. Sounds that seem strange to me. It doesn't matter; soon I'll be out of here. Tomorrow night at the latest.

The thought of hitting the road lightens my heart. With his head tucked into his wings, nestled deep inside me,

Jean-François Vézina-Côté closes his eyes, and I know he protects me from the little crabs that run about when my toes sink into warm sand. I'm not going back to work. In the morning, I won't bother getting up and washing, I'll stay in the foetal position trying to keep warm under the sheets, past the usual time.

Legault will be able to find another roommate; my hard-working angel will see to that. We won't even have to say anything to the Czech. My boss at the tannery will curse and swear, but he'll get over it. My angel will take care of that.

I'll write notes to people. If necessary, everyone will receive a note. I want to leave with a clean slate.

A good sign: the departure went well. First thing in the morning, I spoke to Legault. He was discussing something with the Czech on the stairs. I told them I'd made up my mind and nothing could make me change it. Legault nodded without saying a word, his eyes were sad. The Czech said okay and took off. That was all. I spent the day gathering up my stuff, and by about three I was driving down the road that borders the river.

I had made up my mind to get as far as Gaspé, when just beyond Montmagny the motor went dead. My guess is it's finished. I started to laugh. Sort of a nervous laugh. For a whole minute I sniggered to myself. Something snapped. I don't even want to know what. I don't give a damn. It's a miracle that the chassis hasn't flown away in the wind. I hadn't travelled aboard such an old bucket of rust since the *Victoria Marsh* in '53.

Sitting on the running board I look at my angel's photo. He seems worn out, his colours faded, and the ink has smudged the plastic. I caress his red hair with my thumb. My little cherub, you sport a conventional smile, appropriate to your life before decapitation. I hope you know how lucky you are to float, so pure, in the infinite blue.

Here, night is falling and the birds are fussing about. Do you remember what evening is like, Jean-François Vézina-Côté?

Country smells. The wind brings in its wake the dried leather odour of manure piles and the tannin of sour hay. And the smell of black earth on which things get built. I see an aluminum garage with a basic straightforward blue door, a blue chosen by a little boy. I see families who have finished supper, turning on their colour TVs. I, with my head leaning against the open car door, watch a farmer, neither old nor young, coat open, counting a wad of money. A bill blows away and lands on a pat of cowshit. He doesn't pick it up. I believe he puts his foot in it.

Once before, my idle feet, like now in the gravel, kicked about in the earth, to pass the time. They poked about in the sand of a beach. Not far from Havana. I let the pale sand filter between my toes, drinking yellow rum, as I had been since dawn, from a bottle half-buried to keep it lukewarm. I had no desire to return to the boat. Since I had left my father's house in Saint-Henri, my path had led me nowhere but towards exhaustion and fear of death. I was not happy with my lot.

The amber rum balmed my anguish. I smoked my Players, eyes squinting in the bright sun.

I had made the decision to spend my life right there, my form making its mark in the sand, as lazy as a chained dog. And that's when I saw them. At first I thought they were white spots dancing in front of my eyes from drinking too much, or from lack of vitamins. Then I understood that their colour blended them perfectly with the sand: that's why they looked like a mirage. Around my feet tiny crabs slipped from one hole to another, moving at top speed in every direction, like pale spiders. They popped up from the sand faster than the eye could follow. I was a good-natured Gulliver whose presence stirred up a world of miniature people.

I invented a game. First I threw my cigarette butt a few feet away. As soon as the smouldering fag hit the ground, a minuscule crab appeared at the entry to its hole and waited. In a to-and-fro movement that took but a fraction of a second, the crab made off with the smoking treasure. It was gone.

Bored, I caught a little crab as it came out of its hole and one by one I tore off his pinchers and his claws. Next, I fanned the butt of my cigarette and screwed it into the crab's belly until the claspers at the corners of its mouth stopped moving.

Once it was dead, I squeezed it until my fingers were covered with juice.

Curious little animal that feels nothing.

Oh, this little crab, the colour of a dry leaf, has often come to mind. It even became, for a time, a sort of fellow-traveller in my dreams.

On the beach, with whitecaps in the distance, I made only one resolution for the future: never again would anyone send me to the top of anything. I would be happy to spend the rest of my life as an unshaven man among men. That, my beautiful angel, is how I got the moustache.

A short while after my van broke down, a car coming up behind blinked its lights and stopped. A jovial guy got out. It's late, and in the dusky light, the car looks like a deluxe model.

Providence, my little cherub, my infallible one, providence is not dead after all.

Monsieur Harrisson

Monsieur Harrisson is a nice sensitive man. A nice man surrounded by nice people. He has his wife, Rachel, his son, Eric. Eric is a young man of about twenty. He has Jiri, a meek and mild employee, who looks after monsieur Harrisson's property holdings. In monsieur Harrisson's life, everything has been provided for. But, in 1984, not far from the port of Montréal, things took an unfavourable turn. A stiff opposing wind blew up, intractable, altering his course. A minor little clack on the compass which, as the months went by, would send his ship still only a few leagues from port into a sweet little drift ultimately leading to its loss, frozen in ice somewhere in the middle of nowhere, far from human companionship, a drift leaving him to die, forgotten by the world, stripped clean and naked, flat on the planks, his mug streaming with red mucus. In 1984, monsieur Harrisson entered the warm home of his wife Rachel, his son Eric. Puzzled, dumbfounded, perhaps disappointed, for he had just learned that he did not have high cholesterol. Nothing had changed in his medical report: the blood count was, as always, within essentially normal limits; for the rest, he was borderline pre-diabetic, and his psoriasis varied according to the season, the desserts he ate, his stress level, the number of thoughts he repressed. He was coming in from his doctor's appointment when he received a call from the secretary of the Gingras Agency. The ring of the telephone made him jump. Renaud Harrisson is a very sensitive man.

It was with his brother-in-law Gilles Gingras that Renaud Harrisson had founded the small detective agency towards the ends of the sixties. Gilles, an electronics wiz, crazy about gadgets, was endlessly arriving from Seattle, Chicago, Cincinnati, weighed down with new ideas and black boxes heavy as anchors. All those gadgets with their motley coloured wires elicited a smile from Renaud, for whom the agency represented, above all, the occasion to drop his legal studies, studies he had undertaken so as not to go to police school. The agency co-founders also included Burns (he lasted two months), a determined lawyer who had more ambitious dreams than the deadly boring surveillance work the agency required of him. Thus, for a whole year, Renaud Harrisson and his brother-in-law Gilles ran a shaky business wherein Renaud hunkered down in the soft, fleecy interior of his Ninety-Eight, nibbling his Coffee Crisps, his telephoto lens concealed in a navy windbreaker at the level of his thigh, waiting to take, by surprise, an adulterous woman leaving her alleged piano lesson, or a shady lawyer shaking hands with a vile criminal; meanwhile Gilles, an insomniac, dreamed up expansion projects. In 1972, old father Gingras, who had a crook's flair for industrial real estate, had made Renaud's wife and his business associate rich before their time. Gilles and Rachel Gingras, expecting to inherit one hundred thousand dollars between them, found themselves divvying up, in a state of shock, almost three million dollars worth of holdings and securities. Gilles had convinced his sister to invest her share of the inheritance in the agency. In two years, he told her, they would be in the security business, with the average agency employee wearing a uniform, keyrings heavy as hammers hanging from his belt, and trained to run a console of video surveillance screens. With the aid of this manna from heaven, there would be no end to company growth.

Gilles Gingras celebrated the association, arm in arm, with Renaud. But Renaud didn't feel part of it. He didn't feel comfortable. With his wife and his brother-in-law as principle shareholders, the agency was taking on formidable proportions. Suddenly he was in the position of being a boss with, the first year, maybe some fifteen employees under him. No matter how enthusiastically Gilles explained his project, the turn in fortunes had a sobering effect on Renaud. He hesitated... he wasn't sure any more... he hadn't imagined it like this. They gave him a week to think things over. A whole week. A long week. Renaud thought, he got up late, spent all day in his underwear, thought. He looked sad.

It was the same sadness he felt during his first swimming lesson. The uncle who brought him up helped him decide to take swimming. A man of action, the uncle had declared "In this world, my little Renaud, you have to know how to float. How many ignoramuses perish by drowning..." The next day at the municipal pool, the child was well prepared: the bathing suit with the secret pocket for hiding a key, the nose plug squeezed in his closed fist until he saw if the other boys were using them. He couldn't wait to jump in. His eyes closed, he saw himself slide through the water like a glistening dolphin. He was lined up with the other boys at the twelve-foot end. The instructor, to impress them and give them a shining example of what they could amount to if they worked hard, showed off his diving skills. Double twists, triple twists, somersaults, back flips, arched dives, gliding dives, crossed-arm dives, hands-behind-back dives. The boys screeched with excitement each time he hit the water. Little Renaud's face darkened. He would never be able to do that, pirouette in mid-air. With each acrobatic plunge, the cold blade of trepidation sank in deeper. I can't... I never will be able to... nobody showed me how, I... When his turn came, he froze. All he had to do was jump in the water, get a little wet, a happy little plop, to get started. Renaud sulked, his arms crossed. The instructor, puffing like a seal, asked him if he was taking the course. Renaud backed out of the line-up, shaking his head. He returned on foot to his uncle's house, walking for two hours under the hot sun, his towel wrapped around his waist like a skirt.

As the winds of change blew through the Gingras Agency, Renaud confessed to his wife Rachel, almost snivelling, what his real dream was: he had always wanted buildings, apartment blocks. The security business, alarms, cameras, all that stuff made him tense. He had kept this to himself for too long, and now his discomfiture was taking on proportions that...

— You never told me before, protested Rachel, dismayed and maybe a little guilty. She had never guessed.

Renaud Harrisson wanted a job like his uncle's, a worker who felt at peace rewiring a ceiling light, plastering, painting, hanging a door, moving a doorknob. Real work. Screwing screws and nailing nails. That's what he dreamed of.

Rachel felt bad enough not to hem and haw. She'd bought him his first building on boulevard Dansereau. Eight new apartments. Cash. Done. Renaud's part of the bargain was to stay on at the agency. Nothing major: a little surveillance job once a month to keep his name on the payroll, for benefits and tax purposes... To, as Rachel put it, look after his interests there. Just once a month. Sometimes, maybe there would be nothing at all. That was the agreement. Knowing that he could spend the bulk of his time wearing dirty baggy overalls, and revelling as much as he wanted in the aisles of hardware stores, Renaud had not said no.

And in his office in the basement, Renaud would keep a huge locked box containing: his deeds, his mortgage certificates, and a big book in which he would keep his accounts up to date, in his own hand, when he had a moment to himself. He could spend hours breathing heavily over fine graph paper, drinking a steaming diuretic herb tea, and sucking on a candy. The safety in numbers. The security of small boxes.

But, one winter day in 1984, Renaud was summoned by his brother-in-law, Gilles. He was told to go and get the rundown for a job with a new client by the name of Aimé Robillard, who lived on rue Delage in Longueuil.

Renaud Harrisson had just come in from the doctor's appointment, feeling unconvinced, suspicious that the tests had missed some anomaly that would show up in the tone of his skin, in the blush of his psoriasis. He pulled off his rust-stained jeans, paying scrupulous attention to his skin texture, running his fingers over every mark, and took a shower. He donned a pale suit and a navy trenchcoat, the belt knotted behind. Then, sitting on the edge of the bed, he ritually cleaned his nails. Time to do the little job for the agency.

The compass needle clicked in a slightly different direction.

Monsieur Harrisson had heard Robillard's name in law school. Towards the end of the fifties, Aimé Robillard had got himself elected mayor of a small suburban town that was subsequently erased from the map by a wave of annexations. It was an open secret that financing practices of his party were illegal. The town's expenses were frequently known to be five times what they took in in taxes and subsidies combined, and they did it laughing in their beards. Just before the new elections, Robillard found himself disqualified for seeking a new mandate by a special law voted in the nick of time by a federal minister, ostensibly with Robillard in mind. In legal jargon, this law had been dubbed "the Robillard Law": it forbade any person with a criminal record from running for municipal office. Aimé Robillard was obliged to rethink his career.

Gilles Gingras had warned his brother-in-law Renaud: only ask what you need to know. Robillard was the kind of client about whom the less you know the better: "Hello. Who are you looking for? Where do you think he is? Do you have a picture? 'Bye."

This is how the wind started to shift for monsieur Harrisson two years ago: by a rather brusque interview with Aimé Robillard in his deluxe residence, a residence covered with long slender bricks, huge picture windows, its L-shape nicely filling the corner lot.

The picture Robillard handed to Renaud was of a dark-skinned stocky man with a moustache. The man might have been taken for a Mexican farm worker had it not been for the pearl grey tweed suit clearly chosen to show off his tanned face and hands. The Hollywood cut, dated, contrasted strongly with his proud way of holding himself. The cufflinks looked like imitation gold ingots.The man had pulled down his starched cuffs so the gold would show beneath the jacket sleeve and glitter in the camera flash.

— Add twenty years, said Robillard, not taking his eyes from the photo.

He described the man as a sincere friend, almost a son, whom he hadn't heard from for nearly two years. He'd disappeared from view. A broken heart, apparently. Having said that, Robillard sipped a mouthful of coffee from his brown mug, which he then put down carefully, and without raising his eyes, signalled to his interlocutor he now knew all he needed to.

Renaud Harrisson held the photo. Daudelin had frank, laughing eyes.

Seeing it wasn't much to go on, Robillard added, with a sigh, the name of an ex-girlfriend, Mona Novak (a Lessard from Verdun), not to be used except as a last resort. Mona

Novak, Robillard added, weighing his words, was a little "disturbed": Be careful not to believe everything she says. Poor woman.

— Messed up by pills, he added coldly. Take her with a pinch of salt.

Renaud Harrisson returned to his car where Jiri, the young Czech he had been sponsoring for a year, was waiting. He had initially hired him to carry his tool kits when he made the rounds of his buildings; now Jiri could do anything. He drove Jiri to one of his buildings on boulevard Rousseau. The tenants in number four had no hot water; the family in two, just under, were crabbing about a leaky ceiling.

— You haven't changed your mind about your name? Renaud asked as they drove along.

Jiri made a gesture implying he wanted to drop it. Renaud thought that the foreign first name of the young man was an obstacle. He had tried to broach the subject from every possible angle, choosing his words carefully so as not to appear racist. It was simple: Jiri would never manage to make friends with a name that didn't sound like it was from here. Monsieur Harrisson had even offered to look after the legal paperwork for Jiri. Gérard or even Gerry was close and sounded better. Each time, Jiri smiled without replying.

When Jiri arrived from Prague, monsieur Harrisson already had six apartment buildings with a total of thirty-eight units and only four vacant. Renaud liked to have his agenda chock full. When he could no longer keep up with the work, he hired a worker, or some friend of his son Eric, but after a while they turned out to be ungrateful wretches. As for Jiri, he wasn't full of himself. He showed up at the Gingras Agency, pale, dark circles under his eyes, possessing only a few words of English, ready to do anything, night watchman at a construction site, porter, cleaner... Monsieur Harrisson liked him immediately.

He took him home and Rachel didn't hide her annoyance. She found the arrangement a nuisance. The new employee's room was the basement billiard room, where Renaud opened out the sofa-bed for him. Eric lost no time in complaining that his billiard shot was deteriorating: since the "immigrant" had moved in with his boxes, he couldn't play any more. As for his girlfriend, Anne-Sonia, who thought she wouldn't be understood because of the language barrier, she laughed outright at Jiri's clothing.

Jiri, feeling ill at ease, had expressed a desire to find a room in Montréal, near boulevard Saint-Laurent, where he had noticed the shops were European. Renaud flatly refused; his employee would be moved to a free room in the basement of one of his buildings, on boulevard Jacques-Cartier, a hop, skip, and a jump from the centre of Longueuil. Jiri's mouth fell open at finding himself the owner of a sofa-bed, a television, a toaster. Plus salary and Christmas bonus.

Jiri does everything for Renaud. Soldering, painting, rebalancing the ballcock in the toilet tank. Sweeping the stairs. Collecting rent. Exactly as he's told. His French is good enough to understand.

Monsieur Harrisson dropped Jiri on boulevard Rousseau. He would be back to pick up his assistant at five o'clock, latest. After, they would maybe go and treat themselves to a pizza. Meanwhile, he would figure out how to flush out madame Novak. So he could find Richard Daudelin. Get the job over with. And go back to his buildings.

Mona Novak had neither telephone nor cable, but a hydro bill in the name of Monique Lessard led monsieur Harrisson to a semi-basement studio on rue Guilford in Montréal. Mona Novak had briefly been a minor star at a private television station. That was already twenty years ago. Now she was finished, her face was emaciated. She wore a wig that was blonde and coarse. It was the end of winter, and her apartment was as overheated as an old woman's.

To get a foot in the door, Renaud had invented a likely story. He was researching a series of articles on the grandest hours of Québec's trade union movement. He was currently working on the biographical notes of the union activist Wilfrid Daudelin, now dead some fifteen years. He wasn't sure what he was looking for: anything, a photo, an anecdote...

Lying turned Renaud on: his heart beat faster when he was playing a role. Sweat drops broke out on his brow, red spots flourished on his neck, and the person he was talking to, concerned by his state, was instantly moved to come to his aid, to give him anything he wanted. On top of that, Mona liked his honest face. As soon as she had been reassured by his research project, she opened her door and heated up some coffee. Renaud sat down at the kitchen table, equipped with a notepad and a ballpoint pen. Mona was a thin, awkward woman who grew nervous around a man. For the third time, she patted a curl into place in front of the little round mirror over the sink. She spilt some sugar and started to giggle like a young girl. With his finger loosening his collar to get some air, Renaud asked her to tell him about herself first, where she came from, what she had done in her life, then they'd get onto Daudelin... He told her that's how he worked: he liked to start with people where they were and work up to the subject. She sat down. She thought, her gaze probing.

— I am a Lessard from Verdun, she ventured. My father...

And Mona broke off.

— Where I come from, Monsieur Harrisson, is really not interesting. Really not. Do you want me to sum the family up in one word? Once, trying to describe them, I came up with the word Nothing. Nothing with a capital N. I sprang from Nothing, she finished, smiling.

— Tell me about yourself.

— You know, Monsieur Harrisson, she told him after a while, it took the time it took to learn to live with the idea, but now I can say it: I am not an amiable person.

And Mona Novak poured out her heart. And Renaud followed right along, listening to her anecdotes, her by-the-bys, her truisms. She had never had a girl for a friend: it was, to her way of thinking, the most bitter failure in the life of an aging woman, worse than the failure of relationships between men and women, which were, according to her, impossible.

Richard Daudelin had never criticized her personality, her highs, her lows.

— I was a bit of a princess, I realize, she owned. But Richard took everything in an even-tempered manner... which maybe amounts to the same as not taking any notice whatsoever...

Renaud kept her on the subject of Richard Daudelin.

Mona explained to him that, during all the years that they went out together, she and Richard had never cohabited. They lived "independent lives." He was, like her, a *loner.**

She described Richard. He was a faithful man, not so much on account of his character type, but because of his skin eruptions. They made him timid around women, and thus, by force of habit, little inclined to run around: he had red patches all over his body, on his back, on his thighs, on his arms, his head, even his private parts. Psoriasis. It came in waves and never completely disappeared. He wasn't supposed to eat dessert on account of that. Once, she had made him a bread pudding, which kept him from sleeping. Scratching all night long and heaving big sighs. Sometimes it got so bad it bled. Mona's sheets were always blood-stained. She didn't notice after a while. It became normal. Like a flecked motif. But, despite all that, she never looked down on him. She emphasized "never." She said she would have made a good nurse.

She moved towards a stand of knick-knacks and porcelain figures and took a framed picture in her hands. She grimaced, a tiny grimace. She ran her thumb over the gold crenellated frame.

— I used to be a personality, on TV, you know, she said, kind of proudly.

She handed the photo to Renaud. It was a faded image clipped from *le Petit Journal* sometime in the sixties. On it, she was smiling during a gala for crippled children, accompanied by Magic Tom and little Sylvain Massé, leaning on his new crutches. Mona was glowing. Refrigerator ads and walk-on hostess gigs at CFCF had got her this mention in the newspaper. Before that she had worked for Bell as an operator and as a cigarette girl in a club on rue Sainte-Catherine. That's where she saw Richard for the first time. He'd asked her for a package of Winstons, but she didn't have any.

— He did it on purpose, she explained, with something like a wink.

Mona's coffee had grown cold. Renaud had already been

in her kitchen for an hour. The red splotches on his throat had grown pale. His heart was almost back to normal.

She asked him if he knew anything about Richard's life now. He replied, with caution, that all signs pointed to the likelihood he had "disappeared." Renaud chose his words to leave the impression that Richard could be dead.

Mona wasn't so sure. In her opinion, Richard was still on the prowl. He kept to himself, but he was around. She could feel it in her guts.

Squeezing her cup with both hands, Mona told him about the May morning she escaped death by the skin of her teeth. Things had been going badly for some time between her and Richard, they saw each other less and less, mostly dinners where neither spoke a word. But nothing "went on" until Rémi Asselin, a jeweller, took a shine to her.

— I don't run around, on that subject I can hold up my head, she said, with affectation. But, let's admit it, I was over forty when I met Rémi. For a woman...

She had spent the night at his place, at Longueuil. In the morning, a chilly spring morning with thick dew on the grass, they left the house. On the steps, she suddenly had to turn around and go back in to get the gold earrings she'd forgotten. Twenty-four karat keepers that Rémi had given her the night before. This absentmindedness saved her life. When the car blew up, she was inside digging under the sofa cushions. The living-room window cracked. Rémi was spared because he wasn't all the way into the car. It's a total miracle he's alive.

Rémi didn't want to have anything to do with Mona after that.

— Normal, she sighed, it was on account of me that it happened.

Surely, she said to Renaud, he'd heard tell of the bombing.

— It was in all the newspapers.

The car was parked across the street, in front of Madame Vézina's. Her son had come over to hang around Rémi. He always did that. He was funny that way: the minute he saw Rémi, he hurried over to him. Children who have no father are needy, Mona knew, but she had never liked that child. Not just because he was a redhead but for all kinds of reasons. She grimaced. She didn't elaborate. She swore she still felt upset when the child had been blown to bits. She told Renaud he couldn't imagine what a mess that could make, a blown-up child. Brains, fingers, bones, all over the place. Mona knew exactly who was behind the hit, but she told the police nothing. Rémi either. After that, she became depressed. She said, "Imagine what kind of life I could have with that hanging over me!" Everytime she saw *Allô Police* in a kiosk, she was afraid her name would be mentioned in connection with the bombing on rue Radisson.

— I talk a lot, she apologized abruptly, putting her fingers over her lips.

— I am here to listen, Madame Novak.

Mona, telling her story, got a little carried away, alternately voicing relief from terror, then voicing terror. Little by little her voice became a whisper.

— I lost my hair because of the bombing, Monsieur. What you see now, it's a wig.

Renaud pretended to be surprised. He assured her that he would have never guessed.

Then she said that the last she heard of Richard was from a friend who claimed she saw him distributing Jehovah's Witness literature at the Berri métro station. That's why she didn't believe he was dead. Mona laughed coarsely.

— But I think she was pulling my leg.

— A friend? pressed Renaud.

— A manner of speaking, she said, embarrassed.

Adopting a calm, principled tone, as if speaking in aphorisms, Renaud said it was difficult to feel close to those one called friends. She looked at him, astonished. The tiny damp room filled with silence. The ticking of the clock, the clicking of the heater, and little creaking sounds filled up the empty space.

On the subject of Richard's father, Mona had nothing to offer. Not one single time had she been taken to visit any of his relatives. Only once had she shaken the hand of "the patriarch" (that's how she referred to Wilfrid Daudelin); they'd run into him by chance, and he had snubbed her. Probably because she was working for English TV.

— No, she sighed, for Richard I was, above all, a source of pride because you could see me sometimes on Channel 12, and, I was convenient: evenings, *he didn't have far to go*, as he told me one night when he'd been drinking. Mona Novak, she said, pronouncing the name with an exaggerated American accent, existed only under the studio lights and in the darkness of the bedroom. Apart from that, you apparently couldn't take me anywhere.

She said "About his father Richard never talked." She wondered if he'd even gone to his funeral; she doubted it.

— I'm afraid I haven't been much help. You must be disappointed, she said, looking him in the eyes.

— Not at all, Madame Lessard.

— Obviously, some things are better not repeated, she said in a very low voice. I know I can trust you, Monsieur Harrisson.

Renaud smiled reassuringly and asked if could use the bathroom.

Mona Novak's medicine cabinet contained a variety of anti-anxiety medication, and moisturizing creams in large economy size. Perfume samples. A basket of soaps shaped like hearts, rabbits, peonies, doves, covered with a pale layer of dust. A jar of bath-oil beads for the bath, sticking together as they collapsed in on themselves. Renaud raised lids, unscrewed caps, smelled.

Mona came and tapped on the door, asking him to go.

— My program's coming on, she explained.

Renaud flushed the toilet and thanked her as he came out. The television was already turned on. She said he could come back when he wished, some other time, to talk. She said it with her finger pushing him in the back to the door. He put his rubbers on in the stairwell.

At the Berri métro exit, monsieur Harrisson noticed neither proselytizer on the street corner nor pamphlet in the garbage can. He wound his scarf around his ears and sat on a bench. He waited, feet crossed. This was the job he liked doing best for the Gingras Agency: at the most one might have said he was lazing about. He knew how to get the job done or cut corners, if he felt like it: the proof, for him, that he was still a past master at the intelligence game.

During the hours he waited, he leafed through catalogues, marker in hand, or ran a mental check-list of the stock in his storage room, an apartment he kept empty for the purpose. Renaud never threw anything out: windows, doors, sinks, taps, bits of pipe, water heater, screens, paint brushes, nails, anything that might be of use in moving a hinge, repairing a window, expeditiously executing a promise made to a tenant.

But on this particular day, sitting on a public bench by Berri métro, Renaud Harrisson was drawing out an easy case.

Mona Novak, he thought, had the electric heating on too

high. She had it on as high as it would go. It was bad for the skin and ruined the bronchials. She reminded him of a certain woman, named Dupras, whom he had followed ten years ago. This woman was very sensitive to changes in room temperature. Her lover had the air conditioning on full blast. Her sniffing started her husband thinking. There wasn't a single picture of the Dupras woman without a handkerchief at her nose.

Sooner or later, Renaud presumed, a Jesus-freak would step up holding out a tract, and give him a lead that would take him directly to the object of his quest without any effort, because that's how things worked in the business. Information always "fell" into your lap. He watched the shivery pigeons squabbling over a French fry. He had no opinion of Richard Daudelin. Nor, apart from the psoriasis, a burden Renaud also had to bear, could he imagine the man "in the flesh."

He thought about Mona Novak, born Mona Lessard. This woman thought that there was no such thing as something you could call a close friend. Could it be, mulled Renaud, that friendship is nothing but a childish thing, like an anecdote that renders you nostalgic? The mature man would have, rather, contacts, associates. If one were to believe this woman, fretted Renaud Harrisson, one would think that those who spoke of friendship were retarded or, simply, liars.

The next day, under scraps of a submarine sandwich in a garbage can at métro Saint-Laurent, monsieur Harrisson unearthed a pale green alcohol-printed leaflet. It was mimeographed, folded in four, titled *In Verity I Say Unto You...* and contained a Bible verse and a brief commentary by someone called Ruth Russell. Renaud would find out more the next Friday at seven p.m. on boulevard Saint-Laurent.

Sister Russell's Mission had instantly made monsieur Harrisson feel ill at ease. The old premises, not very large, on the third floor of a building with storefronts on the ground level, dated maybe from the early twentieth century. The place was okay, except for the floorboards, burned with salt stains and peeling paint on the pipes. The air was damp with coats and boots that made little puddles of melting snow under the chairs. In front there was an industrial grey platform where the woman preacher, accompanied by two young girls in ankle-length old-fashioned dresses, warmed up the audience: one, at the piano, played arpeggio after arpeggio, the other chiming in with organ sounding riffs on the accordion. Sister was a small austere woman with the eyes of a gull, pale and sharp. She took up position directly under a bare bulb dangling from a thick slightly frayed electrical cord. During part of the sermon, Renaud kept his mind busy calcuating what it would cost to fix the place up.

For the rest of the singing and preaching, he scratched the back of his neck, his head. His skin eruptions stung, scaling and burning a little. His wrists itched. When the choir voices rose, he sighed. The woman with the grey chignon was fervid in her denunciation of contemporary morals and there seemed nothing to add to her reciting of Bible verses. But her personality got on his nerves. Like a mosquito flying around in a blind room. That's it, thought Renaud, it's the feeling you'll get stung as soon as you're not looking.

In the second half of the evening, sinners went up on the stage to openly repent. Renaud held back a smile at the gold mine that these confessions might comprise for a greedy informant. I sinned by doing this... I sinned by doing that... I promise not to sin again... I am saved. Frankly intrigued, he couldn't manage to discern the signal that released the chorus of hallelujahs.

He spotted Richard Daudelin. Not a very large man, compact, a solid body, nearly fifty, maybe older. The moustache in the photo was gone. He was sitting three rows from the front, next to a disabled person.

After the faithful were given permission to depart, Renaud followed Richard Daudelin and took down his address. By Monday, he'd know where Daudelin worked, if he worked.

That night, Renaud Harrisson slept badly. He wasn't relaxed. No sooner did he feel ready to drop off, than his psoriasis came to drag him back from sleep, as piercing as long, thin needles. And then, his excema started to well up between his fingers. Rachel sent him to sleep on the sofa because he was tossing and turning too much.

Early in the morning, his son Eric roused him with a dumb question: "Are you getting a divorce?" His voice was indifferent. Renaud ignored him. He had hardly slept. On opening his eyes, what he saw was Richard Daudelin sitting very straight on his wooden chair. How, Renaud asked himself, could a man go from wearing designer tweeds and monogrammed shirts one day to the life of a monk almost, nearly destitute, the next? On his wooden chair, Daudelin floated, as free as a bird, eons from premeditated murder, eons from putting a bundle of dynamite under the hood of a car, possibly dirtying his Egyptian cotton sleeves in the process. For breakfast, monsieur Harrisson swallowed an antacid.

Sunday, Renaud headed for the Mission and remained inconspicuous near the door at the back. He didn't want anyone to get the impression he was a hopeful, and the orating style of this Indian-looking woman turned him off. He didn't stay until the end.

Monday at dawn, he was waiting outside Richard's. He got into bus #55 with him. At rue Ontario they caught the #125 and got off a few steps from the Wescott Tannery. Renaud was surprised such places still existed. He kept his distance. In the unloading area, the manager, gesturing like the pope declaring a new holiday, informed his employees that he had just installed a shower for them. One shower for nearly a dozen men. Most shrugged. Renaud slowed down to listen but didn't linger. Sniffing the air, he hurried on. The stench of the skins emitting from the workshop flowed over the men and stuck to their chests and when they smelled sufficiently strong, the sourness of the tannin glued the stink in place. The employees reeked with it when they left work at the end of the day.

Renaud Harrisson got in touch with monsieur Robillard. He gave him a report containing Daudelin's home and work addresses, and his movements. The agency mailed a bill to monsieur Robillard in the week that followed.

Then monsieur Harrisson called Jiri and took up his normal life again. He chewed lemon drops while making his phone calls.

After the Robillard-Daudelin job, when Gilles Gingras informed Renaud Harrisson that the agency would no longer take private contracts, only institutional or industrial jobs, when Gilles Gingras explained that Renaud would nonetheless be kept on the payroll as a consultant, that it would require nothing of him, that it was, in a way, an honorary title for a founding member, when Gilles Gingras made this announcement, sprinkled with mollifying platitudes, Renaud was not in the least put off. He had his buildings. And Jiri.

Rachel, feeling caught between her brother and her husband, breathed a sigh of relief at Renaud's reaction. The Gingras Agency's restructuring had, once more, gone smoothly.

— It won't change anything between us, Renaud reassured her.

In an intimate moment, she confessed she would miss the outfit. The blue trenchcoat. The pale vest. She thought it clean-looking. She liked it when Renaud wore a tie, nice clothes. Well-groomed and handsome.

They made love. He slept well.

Next morning, monsieur Harrisson awoke, free of the Gingras Agency. He breathed a sigh of relief. It was like a breath of fresh air in his life. As free as Richard Daudelin, he thought. These thoughts came with his hands clasped over his heart, the comforter pulled up to his throat. Rachel had been up since dawn.

Towards eleven o'clock, Renaud, sitting on the edge of the bed, munched a Coffee Crisp he'd left half-eaten in the drawer of the bedside table. He took an over-large bite, chewed as best he could, then let it sit in his mouth while staring at the bedroom wall. He thought of nothing, suspended in time. Saliva filled his mouth to the bursting point. He bounced up and down like a buoy. It leaked out at the corners of his mouth. Rachel came charging in with clothing in dry-cleaner's plastic over her arm.

How are you? she inquired chirpily.

He forced himself to swallow with a smile. She smiled back.

The Saturday following his change of status at the Gingras Agency, monsieur Harrisson gave himself a day off, asked Jiri to make the building rounds on his own. For an hour, he drove around Longueuil, aimlessly, whistling a little tune, and absentmindedly tapping his finger on his camera, hidden under a bag on the seat. Then he crossed the bridge. He had decided to pass the day in the vicinity of the port, to spy on Richard Daudelin and maybe take a few shots of him.

Renaud, with his camera hanging from his neck, where everyone could see it, looked like a lost tourist.

Richard was there. He was wearing a pair of ochre pants made of wide-waled corduroy, clean but a little short, a houndstooth patterned windbreaker with faded elbows. His shoes were thrust into rubbers with the limp bow of a brown shoelace sticking out. Renaud took a series of photos: distance shots. Back shots from top to toe. Then zooming in on details. Different light angles. Serial motion shots. Richard Daudelin's ear. The curved nail of his thumb, gripping a flyer.

The subject was handing out tracts: inviting people to come and hear Sister Russell preach. Every gesture was steady, serene. He didn't try to persuade people. At the corners of his lips played the smile of the successful salesman.

An hour passed, and Renaud, overcome with a childish desire to play with fire, decided to walk by him. He'd go over nonchalantly so Daudelin could hand him a tract that he'd take with a naïve thank you or maybe even astonished gratitude. Renaud put his camera in his bag and walked toward Richard Daudelin.

His heart raced. His neck reddened.

Passing Daudelin, Renaud held out his hand. It was awkward. Bad timing, too sudden. Richard Daudelin shook his hand, smiling, and handed him a bright yellow leaflet. He said, "Jésus vous aime. Jesus loves you."* It was almost whispered, a kind of greeting. Renaud snatched the tract, walked faster. When he looked back, Daudelin was in deep discussion, having already accosted someone else. Renaud stood there waiting for him to look up, convinced there would be further eye contact. But Daudelin did not do as he expected, and Renaud's heart swelled with disappointment. Almost to the point of crying. Why, thought Renaud, why are people like that? It was always the same. Since childhood, as if fate wished him ill. For example, a man would ask him the time. And Renaud told him, happy the man had singled him out. The man, in asking him the time, went so far as to smile and look him in the eyes. They were clearly connecting: a friendly connection. And that's why Renaud had never had friends: he was waiting for that man. Already his head was full of things they would do together. But the man went on without a word, without looking back, leaving Renaud glued to the spot, more alone than before. Why, Renaud asked himself again, do they always do that?

When he got to the corner of the street, the tears sprang forth, suddenly, like a faucet. He sobbed, his closed fist on his breast. He was afraid for his heart, afraid that someone would see him, afraid they might see he'd been crying when he got home. He had an image of himself covered with little windows, and he recited to himself: "Everything must be closed."

Renaud looked at the hand that had shaken Richard Daudelin's. It was weird. His hand burned and the heat, as if he had been injected with camphor, radiated right up to his elbow. He felt worried. He started to shake.

In a state of high nervous tension, he went into a Jean Coutu Pharmacy. He walked up and down every row, slowly, considering the relative advantages and disadvantages of each new product, running his hand over a toothbrush, a bath sponge, a bar of soap, a box of bandaids, until peace returned.

The sweet smell emanating from the rows of products calmed him: a mix of pink detergent, milk chocolate and chalky pills. He also found comfort in the fabulous quantity of bottles with lids screwed tight and sealed for greater freshness, secreting balms full of healing promise for every ailment, from the most common to the rarest.

They were lined up. They were brightly lit. And the ceilings were high.

Monsieur Harrisson bought a white cardboard box with a lock; boxes are always good for keeping organized. And a tin of Valda lozenges.

By evening, back home, a worn-out Renaud Harrisson had regained his calm. In the bathroom, he looked at his forearms. The left one was covered with bright pink scaly eruptions. It was easy to see why. The pecan pie at supper; even as he ate he knew this would happen. As for the right forearm, the one touched by Daudelin (Richard Daudelin with his astonishing body heat), the spots had remained pink, almost pale pink, almost healed. The skin was changing as he watched.

Monsieur Harrisson slept the sleep of the dead, flat out, deep, departed.

In the morning he sat up and stared at the rumpled bed. Until noon. He stayed like that, lost in thought, making an absentminded movement from time to time: he stroked his unshaven cheek, scratched the bone of his nose, gently pinching the skin of his right forearm. The skin was as smooth and soft as the belly of a trout.

Wednesday evening, monsieur Harrisson was at the Mission, posted at the exit, ready to take off as soon as the faithful made the first signs of leaving. Sister Russell has let the breath of the Lord pass through her and Renaud, his arms crossed, hasn't listened. He has stared at Richard Daudelin's head until peace flooded through him, through his shoulders, his soft arms.

One day, he followed him all the way to the tannery. Another day, he shadowed him in the port.

Once he pressed up against him during rush hour in the métro and let his heart rise and fall.

Once, Renaud sent Jiri out to buy a pen from Legault, the disabled man with whom Daudelin shared a flat. The unintelligible disabled man was at his post, on a corner two blocks from his place, with his tray of ballpoint pens. Jiri understood nothing of what he said, a string of vowels without consonants pronounced with the effort of a weightlifter lifting weights. Monsieur Harrisson stood back a little, trying to follow their conversation.

Renaud took shots. Different kinds of shots. Daudelin in gloves, piling up the stinking hides that a truck was unloading. Daudelin, his eyes closed, his hand on his heart, meditative, waiting for the bus. Daudelin tying up his shoe. The white cardboard box was filling up with contact sheets.

There were also poorly exposed photos of Daudelin arriving in the port with Legault. They each worked in their own spot for the distribution of tracts, but for the distribution of Bibles in the port, they worked together. It was Legault who, with his halting uncertain gait, lugged the box. Richard Daudelin preceded him, looking almost proud. He was the donor. Monsieur Harrisson had pictures of that.

After a zealous month in which Jiri took on increasing responsibility, monsieur Harrisson woke in the night, all aglow with a plan. He went down to his office in the basement and called his employee. It was two o'clock in the morning.

—Jiri, he whispered in a rather grave voice, we are going to become the owners of a new building.

And monsieur Harrisson bought, for an exorbitant price because he didn't know how to conceal his eagerness, the mixed residential and commercial building where Richard Daudelin rented his room. To get the required downpayment, he sold off a very respectable block, without consulting Rachel.

The acquisition of this decrepit, cockroach-infested property, with its clearly rotting beams and dangerous gaps in the upper-landing floor had become the central preoccupation in monsieur Harrisson's existence. Jiri couldn't believe his eyes. But his boss offered no explanation.

The first thing that Renaud did was to move out the lodger occupying the room next to Daudelin's.

— We'll be needing a new storeroom for small stock items, he explained. We'll put them in here, in stacked-up boxes.

— Kind of unhandy, all the buildings are in Longueuil, a fair distance, commented Jiri.

Monsieur Harrisson didn't listen. The store room plan excited him.

On one side of the wall, Daudelin slept, prayed, ate. On the other side of the wall, there was an empty room. Next, maybe a shelf of nuts and bolts, a box of faucets, a pile of doors. Then a chair. Monsieur Harrisson wasn't consciously intending to go there a lot but it permitted him, if he wanted, to sense the proximity of Daudelin, to let himself give sway to the pounding of his heart, to wallow in the soothing heat that flowed over the remaining blotches on his skin.

One morning, while Daudelin was at the tannery and Legault was at his post with his tray of pens, monsieur Harrisson let himself into their apartment with his new key. The place was shabby. The wallpaper was peeling in an upper corner. The dishes stacked in the drainer were badly washed. The linoleum was lifting. Water stains dirtied the top of the walls. Renaud, embarrassed, looked around.

Richard's shirt was on the back of a chair, darned at the elbows. Plain white cotton speckled with blood. Renaud empathized. Oils, sunlamps, bandages, nothing prevented the lesions from cracking and spotting sheets, undershirts and underpants. The brand of one's yoke only fades with time. Richard fingered the cloth, fondled it. Power passed through it. Like fog that dims sharp edges. It felt warm.

The undershirt, in a heap on the chair, was also stained with old blood.

There was something in the pocket of the shirt. A newspaper clipping with a faded picture. A pale little boy, smiling. In protective plastic casing. On the back, on the folded up cut-line was written: *Jean-François Vézina-Côté, 14 years old, an innocent victim.*

On a kitchen shelf, a large jar held change and several two-dollar bills, folded in four; Renaud was touched by the modus operandi. A penny-jar. What children did. It made him smile. He added a two-dollar bill, folded like the others.

Then he walked around the kitchen, his heart full.

He left, groping the key. That evening he wrote a welcome letter to Daudelin and Legault, informing them they had a new landlord. He made Jiri sign the letter.

On the patio that overlooked the swimming pool, monsieur Harrisson watched Anne-Sonia, his son Eric's girlfriend, do lengths. He couldn't imagine how tragic it must feel to lose one's child so suddenly. Someone you were close to since the earliest moments of their being, one of your nearest and dearest, born of you, then bang, they no longer exist. Worse than the worst thing imaginable. Anne-Sonia glided perfectly through the water and emerged, intact, sleek as an otter. She was a well-built girl with white teeth, square-cut bangs and sturdy shoulders; a young woman with a nice clean chlorine smell. When Rachel had suggested to her that she come and stay with them while going to school, Anne-Sonia squealed with joy. Her goal was to one day get a degree in physical education. For her, everything was already decided.

Young Vézina-Côté, he'd blown up. Blown up, Renaud repeated to himself without being able to picture it. Richard Daudelin always had the picture on him and Renaud was perhaps the only person in the world who knew it. He had looked into the pocket of his shirt and he had seen it.

We are united in this knowledge, thought monsieur Harrisson. He guessed Daudelin's remorse. He pictured it.

Monsieur Harrisson took out the navy trench-coat again to visit Jean-François Vézina-Côté's mother. Again, his business card was that of a journalist. The subject: an article on innocent victims. The angle: life after tragedy.

The lady's bungalow had a "traditional" façade: round stone fronting part way up, and the rest aluminum siding simulating clapboards. The yard was richly landscaped: in the middle, perennials proliferated around the cleanly sawn stump of an evergreen.

Madame Vézina was a woman "out of synch," numbed by tranquillizers. She wore a lilac pullover with sequins down the front.

She lived alone. Her jaw compulsively worked as if trying to decoat her tongue with her teeth, but she recounted without hesitation. She owned up at once to Renaud, in a matter-of-fact tone, that Jean-François had the "bad habit" of getting into the cars of strangers.

— I think it's useless to dwell on details, she said with a helpless shrug. Anyway, these days, it's so common...

Renaud found out that Rémi Asselin (he'd moved since then) had been more than kind to Jean-François: bracelets, gold chains, bracelet charms. Even a watch.

— Do you want to see? she asked.

— That isn't necessary, Renaud replied calmly.

She was already on her feet, rummaging around in a shoe box. She handed him the objects, one by one. She had never wondered why these presents were given. She never mentioned them to anyone. Now it's clear to her it isn't normal.

— You don't get something for nothing, she said, as if to herself.

She paused over a lovely ring, then said that the hardest thing was seeing the blown-up bits of her boy. Impossible to clean off the tree. Part of it burned in the explosion. Policemen in overalls shovelled the brain and other body parts as well from the sidewalk. After that a neighbour cleaned up the rest with the spray-nozzle of his hose. The car window had blown right out. She found Jean-François' medal in the geraniums.

She was sleeping when it happened. Since then, she hasn't been able to get it out of her mind that if she'd gotten up earlier, he might have stayed in with her and he would be alive today. Irony of ironies, now she has to take sleeping pills.

— My mouth is always dry, it really bothers me...

Renaud told her there were excellent herbal remedies for

the nerves. She looked at him and said that with monsieur Côté, her ex, things had been off and on. Since the accident, they were off. She had seen a psychologist: it didn't help a bit.

— Obviously, as far as the bomb, nobody knows who planted it, she said, trying to get him to empathize.

Renaud excused himself. He had to go.

— The last door on the right, she sighed.

The bathroom was done up in dark colours. The long counter was made of imitation black marble and a thick purple carpet surrounded the base of the sink. Renaud put his hand into a shell-covered box and found some suppositories. The water in the toilet bowl was indigo and on top of the tank, a pot-pourri of dyed flowers gave off a decided odour of purple candy. Hanging over the basin was a mobile of stars made of cinammon sticks.

While he pissed, Renaud took in the mobile, blowing on it to make it move. Like bits of rust blowing about in the air, he thought. Suddenly, the door opened. Madame Côté came in, simply to continue their conversation. Renaud jumped and moved one of his shoulders forward to try and turn his back on her. He hid his penis by putting his hand over it, as best he could under the circumstances. Madame Côté sighed, her arms crossed: too bad she had chosen black marble. It was hopeless to keep clean. Every speck of dust showed, if not immediately wiped. She sucked in her saliva constantly. "That" (she threw a glance at the cinammon-stick mobile), Jean-François made it at school. Renaud was afraid he would drip on something. Nervously, he made an appropriate comment about her son's being good with his hands, and he put it back in his pants without shaking it.

— I was getting ready to wash the tiles around the bath when you came, she told him. That was my program for today.

Back in the living room, Renaud, hoping she wouldn't ask why, requested a picture of Jean-François. He said he'd make a copy and return it to her. From a drawer in the buffet, she took out a sheet containing several colour photos. They were in the two-by-three inch format, in neat rows. She snipped out one for him with a pair of sewing scissors. She was having difficulty breathing.

— You can keep it. I have lots. Do you want one of me as well?

— It won't be necessary, he replied, pretending to think about it first.

— Promise to send me a copy of your magazine, the mother said. Reading, I like to do that.

In response, Renaud smiled. When he stepped out, she invited him to come back when he wanted. Between one and four, that was the best time.

Monsieur Harrisson had the photo laminated on a thin piece of wood. To make it nice and firm. He locked it up, in his white cardboard box.

One day, monsieur Harrisson tracked down Rémi Asselin. The fat man with dyed hair was coming out of an old factory that had been made over into a male bathhouse. He limped and his hair was still damp. He was just as Renaud expected: complete with shiny bracelets, thick rings, a little crucifix pendant set with a ruby. On seeing him, Renaud immediately gave up on the idea of approaching him. He watched Asselin climb into his car, close the door with effort, and he longed for the calm splendour of Richard Daudelin.

Now that he had the picture of little Vézina-Côté in his possession, Renaud wondered what Daudelin's reaction would be if he gave it to him. Renaud had something for him, something with which he could impress him, that would leave him flabbergasted. He pictured the look on Richard's face. *Oh thank you Harrisson, thank you Renaud,* Daudelin would say over and over, a hand on his shoulder, a warm hand on his back. Renaud would tell him how he had gone about getting the picture, would describe the scene. They would talk over a beer. Laughing. Together. Renaud's skin would prickle with shooting sensations. Healing, Renaud well knew, hurts.

He went into a Jean Coutu drugstore to buy a bag of mints, some vitamin E, some cotton swabs, and bubble bath with seaweed. He walked out, calmed down. The air in the street felt good.

That evening, Renaud Harrisson fell asleep late: Daudelin as usual. Plus his son Eric, who shut himself up in his room, slamming the door. To celebrate his twenty-second birthday, Rachel had decided to cancel his debt to her for the payments she was making on his car. Renaud had agreed with the plan. Even Anne-Sonia had kept it to herself, which they had taken for approval. It was a way, they thought, of making Eric owner of his car. He hadn't concealed his disappointment. He claimed that was no real present. For it to be a present, it had to be a surprise, something new, he reasoned, exasperated, as if they were thick in the head. The car was *not* a present. Anne-Sonia immediately took his side. Rachel and Renaud sat there dumbfounded.

During the night, Rachel pondered ways to make amends. Renaud bit his lip, his thoughts elsewhere. Daudelin again.

The next day, Renaud Harrisson got Jiri to buy some pens from Legault. In the process he was to hand him a bag with a Jean Coutu logo, filled with toiletry articles. As usual, Jiri did exactly as he was told.

Legault got all worked up at the sight of Jiri. He spoke to him. Laboriously. He only wanted to say thanks for the bag and also for the care with which he was looking after the building. Legault took Jiri for the best landlord in the world. Jiri didn't seem to catch a word of what he said: he stood there nodding his head, on the lookout for a chance to terminate the conversation.

Monsieur Harrisson rejoiced in the idea that Daudelin might benefit from the ointments and oil-of-tar shampoo.

During the year, monsieur Harrisson had sold off three buildings and procrastinated or took indifferent care of those that remained. Jiri's responsibilities had grown, and he was now writing a cousin in Prague, trying to convince him to emigrate to Longueuil. Renaud spent his free time trying out ointments on himself, and, once they got his sign of approval, passing them on to Daudelin through the medium of Jiri, who gave them to Legault, who, not knowing what to do with them, in turn gave them to Daudelin, who, deep in a Bible verse, understood more or less what Legault was trying to tell him. Renaud also cooked up a scheme for getting them a new fridge.

And Renaud unearthed a used van that he sold Richard, through Jiri, for fifty dollars.

Richard Daudelin had become Renaud's main preoccupation, his work of art. Pictures of him amassed in the white cardboard box, filled to the bursting point.

During his visits to the Mission, Renaud stared at Daudelin's bent head. He kept his distance. His visits were erratic. Once, he dozed off.

Little by little, in the room he'd kept for himself, the storeroom for small items, vodka libations were introduced, the practice of silent inebriation. Renaud bought a forty ouncer with the intention of giving it to Jiri, then started drinking it with the firm intention of replacing it, then drained it resolutely, sitting on the ground, his legs stretched out in a V-shape, his back against the dividing wall, two feet from the mattress where Daudelin was praying. Renaud awoke in the wee hours, wild-eyed. He went home, bloated, sat a long time in his parked car in front of the house, his windows down, breathing in the early morning air, to look composed. At last, he went in.

— Those Czechs really know how to hold their liquor, he said by way of explanation, to Rachel, smiling slightly to make light of it.

Rachel sulked a little, then plunged into her own affairs. On the home front, there were complications regarding the enlarging of the swimming pool for Anne-Sonia's swimming course.

One evening at the end of summer, monsieur Harrisson turned up at the old Mission, lurking in the doorway. Daudelin seemed nervous. When the testifying began, Daudelin, to Renaud's astonishment, headed toward the platform. He took his time, raising people's expectations. But once he stood up there in front, he was disappointing. His face sagged, and he stayed glued to the spot, as the minutes ticked by. The sister thanked him, a little ironically. That surprised Renaud, irony coming from her. Daudelin returned to his seat and stared at the ground, looking glum, for the rest of the evening. He sprinted home.

Renaud Harrisson spent the evening in the neighbouring room, the storeroom for small items, both hands on his nail gun, taking aim at a paper cone propped up at baseboard level. The little headless nails hit the wall and rebounded, brightly, in the dustballs and sawdust. He shot the nails, one after the other, stopping only for swigs of vodka. The tool's clacking resonated throughout the room. Outside, the murmur of traffic on boulevard Saint-Laurent sounded vaguely festive.

The days were over when monsieur Harrisson returned home at night exhausted, his fingers sticky with silicone, his fingernails tinted with paint, or his hair whitened with paint bits from a window he had scraped until he was ready to drop; the days were over when he opened the door, kissed Rachel, and fell into a dead sleep before he could apologize for his grubby state. On this particular evening, monsieur Harrisson had his ear glued to the wall, but not a word was spoken in Daudelin's bedroom.

His bottle empty, monsieur Harrisson snored in a thick torpor, his head leaning forward, large drops of drool dripping from his mouth. He stayed there, prostrate, until Jiri came to fetch him during the night, making him vomit, dragging him to his car, and driving him to his southshore bungalow.

Arriving in front of his boss's house, Jiri took note of the lights on in the living room and changed his mind: he trundled Renaud home to his place and let him collapse, unconscious, on the sofa.

In the morning, Daudelin broke the news of his sudden decision to move on to Legault, who spoke of it to Jiri, who, for once, seemed to pay attention, to listen patiently. They were in the stairwell. Daudelin was going to New Brunswick, leaving everything behind. He would go and tell his boss, at the tannery, come back, eat, get his clothes, that was all there was to it. He had reason to believe that the Mission, with its imminent move, was drifting away from its former principles. Down there in New Brunswick, said Daudelin, there was a more orthodox community for whom the Word of the Lord still meant something. He'd heard about it and he was going to have a look.

Jiri smiled.

And he ran to tell his boss.

— The tenant is leaving. The tenant, he repeated, miming a communicant, his hands folded.

Jiri summed up Daudelin's plans while Renaud undressed, on edge. He took a cold shower.

Jiri smoked a cigarette, sitting at the table. He entertained himself by moving the cigarettes around the ashtray with a burnt match.

— Things are going to change around here, he intoned, to himself, in fluent French.

Renaud Harrisson returned home at full speed. He was in a state. In his bedroom, he spread pharmaceutical products out on the bed. Tablets to settle the stomach, laxative pills, a hemostatic stick with a granular tip, an anti-inflammatory ointment, a tube of liniment of camphor, eye lotion with mineral salts encrusted around the dry opening.

Garlic capsules, a little stale. A tiny jar of vaseline, unopened.

Cough syrup. Pills. Talcum. And as well, in the higgledy-piggledy, some tranquillizers.

And the red pillbox, the toothbrush, the enema, the soapbox with its soap. Sugarless gum. Rubbing alcohol. You can never be too prepared, Renaud said aloud.

And he took a minute to calm down.

His cases were open on the bed. Three toiletry cases. A duffle bag for clothing. The camera and the white cardboard box. Trying to calm his rapidly beating heart, Renaud breathed slowly from his mouth.

His son Eric came into the room.

— It might turn out that I could end up trying to get into photo school, he announced. Uncle Gilles said he would pay for my equipment.

So his son's vascillating seemed to be coming to an end: at last he was interested in a career. Eric wanted to study. In a flash of recognition, Renaud realized that what his son did was of no interest to him, had been of no interest to him for years. He remembered his son Eric at five, radiant, jumping on him to play. Eric at five, who let him bite his ear, giggling. Eric at five. And the first day of school. Period. From that time on, he drew a blank.

Renaud knit his brows, astonished at the number of bags he had filled.

— You're going on a trip? Eric repeated.

— Yes, that's it. Tell your mother not to expect me for supper.

— Obviously.

— Leave me alone, will you, said the father in a gentle voice, his gaze fixed on his toiletry kits.

Three kits, that was a lot. However, everything seemed indispensable to Renaud Harrisson. You could never be too careful. Who could say if he wouldn't need, say, an antibiotic cream, maybe even in an hour from now, even if he stayed home?

Leaning back lightly, Eric pivoted back and forth around the doorframe moulding. Renaud looked him right in the eye. Heaving a sigh, Eric stopped and left the room. He dragged his feet down to the basement.

Renaud tied up the white cardboard box. It was the type of box you use for filing: made of cloth-covered cardboard, slightly yellowed, slightly dirty. It held pictures, contact sheets, press cuttings, a page carefully torn from *Traduction oecuménique* where a Bible verse had been circled in red and, as well, a bundled wad of different tracts distributed by Richard Daudelin since 1984, some crumpled, others, intact.

Richard quivered with emotion while packing his bags. He walked out, the cardboard box under his arm, on his way to tailing the precariously wired-together van of a man who was leaving his wife behind. Renaud's son was in the basement, insulated by his earphones; his wife Rachel and Anne-Sonia were at the industrial park in Boucherville buying swimming-pool accessories.

Renaud wiped his forehead. "My heart," he thought, "might not stand up to the strain. The Italian syndrome..." He laughed nervously. His palms, flat on his temples, were those of a child wanting to block out the words of his uncle, that old man who thought out loud in the penumbra of his living room, hunkered down in his leather armchair, a glass of gin in his hand. At the construction site, a fifty-five-year-old Italian bricklayer had just died. A fatal heart attack. The uncle spoke categorically, and Renaud, crouched behind the leather armchair, followed the remonstration: Italians are all touchy, wine-drinking over-sensitives. Always laughing about something. Can't stop rubbing each other's backs, kissing each other. And when aren't they crying. Or saying their prayers in broad daylight. They're embarrassing and only make everyone uncomfortable. It's not surprising that a heart, worn out by all those nerve-wracking emotional outbursts, should give up. For monsieur Harrisson's uncle, it was normal that Italians died of heart problems.

At his place, Daudelin had gathered together a few clothes, his Bible, and he hung around a little. Two pieces of toast with cheese, a coffee, a moment of meditation, his hand on his heart.

Towards two o'clock in the afternoon, he threw a canvas kit-bag of clothes in the back of his van and pointed the steering wheel towards Acadia. He'd drive along the river until he found a place to stop, go with the flow. As the mood took him.

Renaud Harrisson rushed over to boulevard Saint-Laurent and waited. The navy trench coat in a pile on the back seat covered the white cardboard box. He shaved in the car, sipping a thermos mug of coffee. When Daudelin started out, he followed. At first, it was at a distance. But on the road along the river, he wasn't playing around any more: Renaud no longer refrained from following right behind. The van didn't exceed the speed limit. All the other cars passed it. Renaud remained faithful.

Just as Renaud Harrisson fervently wished, Richard Daudelin's van broke down. On the 132 between Montmagny and L'Islet, on the edge of a farm. The van slowed, and came to a halt. Daudelin opened the door, swung out his legs, and sat there. A little like Rémi Asselin likely did, guided by his own personal guardian angel, one providential second before the explosion.

Renaud Harrisson put on his hazard lights and got out of his car. He slowly walked over. He was trembling and was afraid it would show. He was sorry he hadn't had a drink to act more natural. The setting sun, the dim twilight, set his nerves on edge. He walked towards Richard Daudelin, who got up when he saw him. This time, Renaud Harrisson would not be left in the background, abandoned, lonelier than ever.

I am going to him, thought Renaud, and when he goes to reply, his full attention will be on me, face to face, his voice speaking to me, for me alone.

He felt a heavy pressure in his damp temples that thumped all the way to the palms of his hands.

— Sir? asked Renaud with a determined joviality, an affected good humour. Can I help you?

Richard Daudelin smiled at him.

Scant hours later, monsieur Harrisson reached the end of his trajectory, a lost creature, breathing his last breath under the loud cracking of clubs, like a whale whose form suddenly flattens after hours of being beached, his lungs collapsing under the tonnage of his blubber.

On the cold carpet of the motel, monsieur Harrisson is stretched out, his arms spread open, his mouth agape, and his head, as glistening as fresh meat, is attracting flies.

A Little Dirt Under the Fingernail

When the tall man stopped on the highway, I thought he was sent by heaven. Without looking twice, I got in. I grabbed my kit-bag of clothing and I got in. I let him pay for my supper in a restaurant. I accepted his offer of a motel. We were brothers. Both of us suffered the same skin problem. As he drove, the man rolled up his sleeve and showed me a pink patch on his forearm. He complained about the traces psoriasis left on his shirt collar. I recognized all the signs. We talked about the arthritis in our knees, the way the pain changed according to the weather. We discussed blood pressure, diabetes, cholesterol.

The man quoted psalms to me; he made mistakes. He said Job for Jacob. I smiled. I saw he was a good man. I felt good myself. I agreed with everything.

It was dark when we arrived at the motel. At the reception desk, while I was examining a rack for brochures, the receptionist, an old boy with a red face and dirty glasses, smiled furtively. At the time, I paid no attention. The tall man had offered to pay for me, it was an understanding. He had explained to me that he had to pay for a room in any case, for he never drove at night. He took out his wallet and paid cash. And the receptionist smiled again. It was my impression that he winked at me. It could have been a nervous tic. I really didn't know. But I couldn't get rid of an uneasy feeling.

When we got to the room, the man wanted to take his shower. He was jubilant. He was singing, and I sat there, on the edge of the bed. My head was spinning, or it was the motel that was pitching. The receptionist's wink had bothered me. I sat there feeling weird. I started thinking over what had just happened. And I remembered that Sister Russell, the Sister of the early days, used to call on us in each sermon to face "the cruel truth,"* the cruel truth, that I had always translated in my stubborn head by "the crude truth," which, for reasons beyond me, rang truer in my mind. On the edge of the bed, while the man took his shower, I examined the crude truth. What had been going on? I grew dismayed as I took a closer look at the situation. The car... The restaurant... It was hard to believe the things I'd heard from that man. His witty remarks. His allusions. Our mutual eruptions of ecxema. The stages of treatment. Every little thing. Always corresponding exactly. One thing after the other.

It was too perfect.

It felt like a bad dream. Or else a test. He had been put there to try me. I looked for a sign, and, like an idiot, I expected it to jump out from a chair cushion, an air-conditioning grill, the stiff, opaque pleat of a curtain.

The man in the big car had been buttering me up. And while I sat here examining the crude truth, he was humming under the shower. A happy tune. For him, this was normal behaviour.

And, behind his counter, the receptionist with the dirty glasses was likely still smirking.

The hotel furniture began to weigh down on me, all around, and I began to feel heavy, too. This, I knew, was a bad sign.

We'd had steak for supper, and then gone right back to the motel. We had spontaneously agreed to leave the next day, at dawn. For Gaspé. He was also going to Gaspé. Our plans coincided. We agreed on everything. It made me dizzy.

Hardly was the motel room door closed than the man with the swanky car had taken off his huge trench coat. Then he removed a camera from a shoulder strap bag. With an insistent familiarity. A sweeping gesture, performed expressly for me. He put the camera down on the television. It made a noise. The thud, heavy as brick, on a wiggly piece of furniture. It was a small camera, equipped with a long thick lens. It looked like a black telescope mounted on a cube. It was gross. He put the thing there, right in my face, left it as if displaying it on its socket. And he waited. He likely thought

I was going to make eyes at him. Say I liked it maybe. I don't believe he could see I was suspicious. Proud of the thing, he started talking about it, as if I'd asked. In an apologetic tone—he even blushed— he avowed he used to be a detective, that he'd had to tail me. He was the guy Aimé Robillard had hired two years ago. It was the clues that Mona Novak let slip, unwittingly, that had led him to me.

And then, long after the contract was finished, he'd kept on my tail, that's all, feeling an affinity. He repeated the word contentedly, mouthing it as if he'd found it after years of searching: *Affinity*.

He had taken pictures of me, in the port, in the loading yard at Wescott, with Legault, hauling a box of Bibles. If I wanted, he would show them to me. There were some good shots. There was one where a pigeon stood on my foot while I handed out a tract. Once, he shook my hand; it didn't matter if I didn't remember. Later he would show me his file box. Everything was in a box.

He knew my van wouldn't hold up all the way to Gaspé, he even—he admitted it— kind of hoped it wouldn't. It was a *big thing for him*, meeting me at last.

I swear I'd never seen this man before I saw him getting out of his car.

While he spoke he was taking off his clothes and throwing them on the chair. When they were all there in a heap, he showed me his back. Were his lesions bigger than mine? Did he bleed more than I did? And he stepped into the shower, singing away. I sat there, trying to rise out of my stupor.

I scratched my ear, staring into space. I rubbed my thumbnail against my worn down teeth. I was starting to see the crude truth: my worst skin lesions are on my inner thighs and my back. How had he known that? How did he know the things he knew? How far had he got with Mona? Did they, he and Mona... Had Robillard become his confidante? Did Legault know him? Maybe Legault was in leagues with him.

The big guy got out of the shower without drying himself. He walked around in his birthday suit, clearly delighted at the way things were going. This was when I noticed his girth. I got the full monty. I sat back and took it all in. He was tall, fleshy. As square as a cop. The skin pink and tight, platinum body hair, and the blondish hair on his head was spread thinly across his pate. Broad cheeks. His lips, pink and full, never quite closing when he talked. He leaned over his pile of clothes.

— I have something I think you're going to like, he told me, looking in his shirt pocket.

And he handed me a picture. It was the picture of a redheaded boy. The colours were clear.

A bright shiny picture. You might have said *new*.

Yeah, Fatso held a school photo in his hand, a glossy photo with a purple background covered with turquoise zigzags, and a kid's smile, a smile sweet enough to open papa's or mama's wallet. He gave it to me. I cupped the glossy photo in my hand, and the big guy stood there wriggling and twisting, as proud as could be, waiting for me to say something, he'd waited *so long for* a word from me.

The laminated picture fluttered from my hand, and I felt cold. The big guy, troubled, covered his stomach with part of a towel. He spoke. It wasn't any louder than an echo. He asked "You don't like it?"

I didn't answer. I grabbed his camera and the heavy lens came unscrewed. I weighed it in my hand like a big grenade. I held my breath and pursed my lips. I raised my arm. I aimed for his head, the marbled temples, the straight hair, the chubby cheeks. I scoured his face for the feature, the small vein, the blotch that would inspire me to act.

As for him, he wasn't afraid. Just a little surprised. He had wound himself in his towel like a Roman stepping out of a steambath. Water drops glistened on his scarred skin. His smelled strongly of ointment. A reeking mix of petroleum and mint.

When my gaze stopped between his eybrows, I hurled the thing hard enough to make him cry tears of blood, but he warded it off, and the lens crashed into the wall and rolled across the carpet.

The big guy tightened his towel and stepped toward me with angry eyes. He muttered "After all I've done for you, Daudelin..."

And right there and then, the veil was ripped open. Fatso raised his finger in the air and revealed all. He shouted out the complete list of goodies, which he'd only alluded to with measured little insinuations up to now. The brand new toaster one morning in the kitchen was him. The bottles of tar shampoo, that was him. The bag of groceries handed to Legault, where do you think they came from? How did Mona Novak's address get onto the Mission mailing list? Christmas, last year, the cash bonus at Westcott, why was I the only guy to get one? He repeated that, as if I were an imbecile. He'd bought the apartment building where I roomed. He was my landlord, not the Czech. His voice rose. He spluttered. He pointed his fat finger in my face.

With my thumb, I scratched the camera casing.

And, as in a power failure, the soundtrack was cut, leaving me in cold peace, sheltered from his meanness. Fatso became a pan in a film shoot. I saw him getting all worked up with his examples, but they no longer touched me. His white cape spread like a wing, following the movement of his arm. I forced myself to think about the little boy in the glossy photo. I was no longer sure of his name. At the most, I remembered a vowel, an agreeable, caressing sound I liked to utter. It seemed to me the little boy's story contained a tree. There, on the picture on the ground, the child was all brightly coloured and he smiled, cold as a window pane. Sealed in his colours. Never again would I be able to speak to him.

When Fatso, in his delirium, put his pink foot on the child's face, walked on it, without looking, I jumped him. To smash his skull with his apparatus. He fell backwards and I sat astride him, pounding. Solid bashes to the forehead. The temples. In the eye. On the bridge of the nose. The skull. He was covered with places to chop. I struck with everything I had. When he no longer moved, I went back to the eyebrows, applying myself to splitting every millimetre open, until the eyelids fell off by themselves. I shouted myself hoarse battering his carcass with the black box. I made, I believe, a decent job of it.

When I had finished, I stayed a moment astride his sunken chest, and let the ferrous scent of his lacerations fill my nostrils. I felt good. Alone.

I stayed there, sitting on him for I don't know how long,

rocking slightly back and forth, relaxed, like a buoy in a soft breeze. I swayed, humming, trying out the first notes of a tune, always coming back to the first note. I quivered. A low sound, as if the wind were blowing through a rusty barrel.

I, Richard Daudelin, in a motel, suddenly, see the crude truth, take strong action, and feel good about it. I, a man whose heart has known ecstasies that made him at one with the universe. I who, moving in the densest crowds, have given of my love freely. I who have exposed myself, like a lizard, to that light that fades all others, even all the miseries of my childhood, from the trivial to the irrevocable. I, in a motel, unexpectedly, have acted in strength, and my act has made me happy.

But my fingers were covered with fresh blood. It was sticky and it was turning brown. It was unpleasant. Rummaging in the big guy's suitcase, I found some rubbing alcohol. I cleaned my hands, rubbing down each finger thoroughly. I threw a dozen dark red cotton balls into the toilet.

When I stepped out of the motel, a damp haze rose from the ground. The sun was rising and Fatso's car was covered with dew. I went back in to get his keys. From behind a curtain, the receptionist saw me leave and I was happy that he saw me with keys in hand. I jiggled them so they caught the light.

I drove for a few minutes in a northerly direction. The light of day grew rapidly stronger. Everything in this huge car was luxurious. Rich. I settled deeper into the plush.

Of all my sufferings, my arthritis is what has made me wince the most. There will be no end to this cross I have to bear. The pain encircles my neck like it's tied in a slipknot, and makes my old man's knees crack. No matter how padded and comfortable Fatso's car was, down to the smallest detail, the accelerator sent shooting pains up my leg, the brake pedal nearly killed me. It was unbearable.

Near a little wooded area, I got out and walked, dragging my feet. My soles scraped along the gravel. I'd never moved like that, not even after coming down from the mast, clutching Grégoire's hard arm, not even at my most drunk on a Cuban beach, never. I had staggered before, I had proceeded at a snail's pace before, but I had never hauled my body along like this.

There was a narrow path leading down the road, whose ruts disappeared into the ferns. A low chain and a PRIVATE PROPERTY sign blocked the way. I stepped over the chain, shaking, and I went, with my pain, into the damp shadows spotted with sunrays. The path seemed empty and I wanted peace, emptiness and peace. Dead peace.

But the forest was swarming with things. It moved. There were orange butterflies, chipmunks flying from one branch to the next, crows shaking their feathers in the underbrush.

There were green insects who struggled against gravity, scaling the trunk of a tree whose bark was too smooth.

I leaned my forehead against a birch, a sturdily rooted birch, and I felt the solidity of the trunk and the roots infiltrating the rocky ground. It didn't shake or wiggle. It soothed. My hands felt the hardness of the cylinder and my lip stuck to the loose white pieces of bark, taking in their bitter chalky perfume.

The leafy branches rose, filling the white air above.

Grégoire, my rock-solid friend, should have left me there,

on the mast, fluttering in the wind like a flag, or he could have come and joined me, like a nice guy, to turn with me on the axis of the world.

The beautiful photograph of the redheaded child, the photo of the young dead boy, shiny, washable, got left on the bedside table, or else it slid under the bed. The other one, the worn-out one that I had cut out of the newspaper, how many years ago, the one that was always warm, caressed each day by my body *your yoke is easy to bear*, the real photo, is the one I miss. All gone. Left somewhere. Or else maybe Fatso took it, without my knowing, to punish me.

Look at me, I am an old man, and I have nothing to show for it. Not even a child's picture. *Take thee a ram without blemish, chosen among the young.* A reliable guy. An example to follow. Each day that heaven brought put a frank smile on his face.

Here, in the green forest, things breathe and everything trembles with the same rhythm. The sun pierces the clouds of flies, pierces the last mists of morning on the red-blonde strands that fall from the tall pines. There, in this passage barred with light, I see clearly that I cannot move without putting my foot on some form of life. I think about this, the last crude truth: under the ferns on the forest floor, under the carpets of russet needles, there is a an entire world of creeping things and worms. And me? My heavy sole walks on one of theirs. I slaughter. With each step, I crush a nervous ant tending its colony of aphids. A dancing caterpillar. A burrowing flea. The white shoot of a flower. A young sprout, easily snapped.